ROGER PRICE'S

THE

TOMORROW
PEOPLE

HOMO INFERIOR

Nigel Fairs

The Tomorrow People:
Homo Inferior
Written by Nigel Fairs
Published in 2024 by
Oak Tree Books
oaktreebooks.uk

in association with
Chinbeard Books

Editor: Paul Simpson
Commissioning/Sub-Editor: Barnaby Eaton-Jones

The text of this book is copyright © 2024
Chinbeard Books and Oak Tree Books.
The Tomorrow People licensed, with
thanks, from Roger Price

Cover artwork: Robert Hammond
Layout and Typesetting: Joe Larkins

Nigel Fairs

The Tomorrow People

in

HOMO INFERIOR

A Chinbeard Books / Oak Tree Books Original

Dedicated to the real Robert, Andy, James, Johnny, Stevie and Bridget, none of whom are anything like the characters they've kindly lent their names to in this book!

The Tomorrow People

I very much doubt that you've met the Tomorrow People before, because most of them left Earth after it was invaded by an insane shape-changing robot Jedikiah and his mighty Tnawi army, back in 2007. There are unconfirmed rumours that two of them remained: Carol and Robert.

If you met them before the invasion, they would have seemed like ordinary young people, but they were anything but ordinary. They called themselves The Tomorrow People because they were a new stage in human evolution named 'homo superior'. The Tomorrow People had developed incredible new abilities. The process of gaining these powers was called 'breaking out' and happened when Tomorrow People were in their early teens.

Tomorrow People could talk to each other through telepathy using the power of their minds. They could also move objects using their minds, using the power of telekinesis. Their minds also gave them the ability to teleport themselves from one place to another by the power of thought, a process they called *jaunting*. To assist with the complexities of jaunting, they used specially designed jaunting belts which helped them with long distance or complex jaunts. However, if they could see their destination or picture, in their thoughts, the belts were not needed.

While the Tomorrow People had developed these incredible abilities, their evolution had left them opposed to killing. They always sought a thoughtful, peaceful resolution, even to the most aggressive situations. But they never backed down from doing what was right and used stun guns, which rendered their targets unconscious, to defend themselves.

There were other Tomorrow People who left Earth to work with the Galactic Federation on its immense space station known as the Trig. Before Jedikiah and his army invaded the Trig and put an end to their power, the Galactic Federation took a keen interest in Earth and the Tomorrow People, gifting them a living biotronic computer known as TIM. The computer had been installed in the Tomorrow People's base, the Lab, which was built by

John Dixon, one of their first, beneath an abandoned London Underground station. Originally just a meeting place, the Lab had grown and had sleeping quarters and other facilities, allowing for longer stays.

The Tomorrow People continue to guard their existence carefully, knowing that not everyone will welcome this new evolution of humanity.

With thanks to Roger Price and Brian Finch.

THE TOMORROW PEOPLE

HOMO INFERIOR

1: Barr-Byzhan

Life is simple when you're a Byzhan born in one of the Citadels of the Unified Hemisphere. Your First Breath mooncycles are followed by your First Naming Ceremony, then Younghood, during which you are cultivated in an Inculcatal Facility. Then, at Validation, you receive your third name and progress from Younger to Citizen. This is followed by pairbonding, during which you are assigned as a Primary or Secondary Designator. By then your role in Byzhan society is decided; a role which you will hold until you are put into an End of Life Foundation.

Yes, life here is simple.

Unless it isn't.

My first memory is of my Primary Designator ordering me to replace one rhyme with another. I can still see their face, silhouetted against the blinding light of the sun, and smell the gripp smoke on their clothes and on their breath, and feel the sharp sting of their hand against my skin. I can hear my Secondary Designator gently closing the

1

living pod door behind them as they leave us to our business, at my Primary's instruction.

Then come the sacred words and gestures that are etched into every Byzhan's consciousness; seared into mine by that dark figure on that bright, icy cycle in my younghood: our Obligations to The Creator, recounted every dark-cyc by Youngers and Citizens alike. I will come to realise—eventually—that after a while the mindless repetition of the words strips them of meaning, rendering them empty: hollow calls into the darkness to a Creator that no longer listens, if They ever did.

But not yet.

As soon as my Primary is satisfied that I have learnt the Obligations, I am sent to my sleeping chamber, which is where the violence occurs. As for the rhyme that the Obligations replaced, the tune haunts me still. The words that so angered my Primary seem innocuous to me now:

> *Bulderbramble bush, how kind are you—*
> *First suncycle's made you blue!*
> *Bulderbramble bush, your laughter's mellow—*
> *Second cycle's made you yellow!*
> *Bulderbramble bush, how tired you seem—*
> *Third suncycle's made you green!*
> *Bulderbramble bush, don't stop to think—*

Fourth suncycle's made you pink!
Bulderbramble bush, your flowers are red—
Fifth suncycle's made you dead!

I wonder now how I came to know the rhyme, and what it was that so incensed my Primary about it; was it the immoral bestowing of emotion onto vegetation, maybe? They are a model Citizen; they have a respectable job in Population Progress Records, which requires no imagination.

Whatever the reason, I am careful never to repeat it again in their company. I am a Youngest, after all, and keen to please them whenever I see them, which isn't often. I wonder if they realise what I was, even back then. It might explain the incomprehensible act of violence in the darkness; the one that my Secondary assures me was a dream, although I swear to this cycle that it happened.

2: Earth

Sunday 18th October, 2009

Two years after Tnawi warships showered many of its major cities with alien death rays, the inhabitants of planet Earth were starting to live something resembling a *normal life* again. Humanity rose from the ashes of devastation like a phoenix, much as it had done after the Great Plague and the World Wars. There were changes, of course; for a while it seemed that feuds over borders or religions had been set aside, as governments focussed on rebuilding infrastructures and economies. In the United Kingdom, Kent, once the so-called 'garden of England', was now a vast housing estate. The West Country, spared Tnawi bombings (apart from a strategic military base at its southern-most point), became the sole property of moneyed city-dwellers fleeing the ruins of their first homes into second, third, fourth ones, driving the locals out, much as they had done before the invasion.

The post of World President (established out of necessity during those desperate times) lasted hardly longer than the invasion itself. Inevitably, President Godwin's successor was deposed, the one after that assassinated and, in the recriminations that followed, all the tired old rivalries resurfaced and, lacking a common enemy, Humanity splintered back off into its old ways.

The Tomorrow People, whose existence remained invisible to the general population, played no part at all in the reparation of Earth. Only weeks before the Tnawi assault, it had come to light that certain governments were aware of the 'Great Breakout' and were taking action to slow it down, if not halt it altogether. The Galactic Federation, itself decimated by Jedikiah and his Tnawi army, made the decision to lie low here and concentrate instead on rebuilding the Trig (their operations base) and re-establishing order on other Federation worlds.

Although she'd worked her way up to a senior position on the old Trig, Carol elected to be one of the few to stay on Earth, manning the labs in the Federation's absence. As comfortable as her quarters had been on the huge space station, she missed her homeworld. The delicious smell of freshly cut grass; the random chatter of commuters on an underground train or a bus; indulging in superficial magazines and bad television in her flat at the end of the day. Mind you, the flat had gone now, destroyed along with most of Camden in the second wave of Tnawi attacks. The government had found money and labour to erect functional new buildings in a surprisingly short amount of time, but Carol was not on the waiting lists; she was living in the lab, deep below Wood Street station, along with Robert Mitchell, a much younger Tomorrow Person and another of John's protégés.

Even though he was barely out of his teens, Robert had had a difficult life so far (and had been labelled a 'potential risk' by Federation medics who should have known better) but Carol liked him. Ironically, she'd only really got to know him in a dream; during their short time in Jedikiah's UC1 machine, they'd shared nearly a year of experiences. She had happy memories of warm nights by the campfire with Elena, Robert and James, discussing soulmates, life after death, the infinite Universe. Robert had learnt how to play the guitar, composing songs for Elena to sing as the nights drew in. James had talked to God. Carol had… stopped. Finally.

Maybe because that world had sprung into existence out of their shared subconsciousness, Carol felt closer to Robert than she might have done if they'd lived together in the *real* world. She believed that this healing time might most benefit them both away from the more complex responsibilities they'd have on the New Trig. John, Elizabeth and Elena could handle them now. Carol fancied a walk along the river and knew that Robert was keen to see the new Thames Barrier.

She knocked gently on his dormitory door. She could have woken him telepathically but preferred to do it the old-fashioned way.

There was no reply.

She tried again.

'Robert?' she called lightly, realising that she sounded exactly like her mother. 'You awake?'

Apparently not.

Robert? she ventured. Even telepathically her voice had the same patronizingly maternal tone that had so irritated her as a girl.

No reply.

She pulled the door open. Robert's bed was empty, and hadn't been slept in.

Robert, where are you?

Nothing.

3: Barr-Byzhan

Dagre-Tiuh, Sennith 3/0, Suncycle Enneha

My first experience of the 'Not Like' comes long before I realise that I am one.

The Not Like have their parts to play in The Catharsae and they always lose. They are either killed, humiliated or banished at the end of the story, and everybody laughs. I laugh, without actually understanding what I am laughing at. But to a Younger those wild, ugly creatures *are* amusing;

they've obviously never stepped inside a Inculcatal Facility—what other explanation could there be for their animalistic behaviour, their complete lack of emotional restraint?

My Secondary marvels at the accuracy of the Players' performances without any first-hand experience of the Byzhans they are mimicking. The Catharsae propagate every misconception about the Not Like and fuel fear and hatred amongst the Younger from the earliest possible age.

I am taught to loathe myself without even realising it.

The first signs of my being Not Like would be obvious, I suppose, to someone who knew what they were looking for, but not to me. Everything that one experiences as a Younger seems *natural*, until one is taught otherwise. So, when I see a fellow inculcatalist at the Facility, Coell-J, step off the designated walkway into the Wildland—the forbidden area at its side—my instinct is not to raise an alarm but to follow them.

It's my first experience of untamed wildland and I'm enthralled and appalled in equal parts. Wildland has no place in the Citadel. Unpleasant and unkempt as it seems on the vid-casts, none of them prepare me for the intensity and variety of its scents, the damp vibrancy of its touch. Feverfruit trees, twisted into unnaturally uneven shapes, compete for space with dark, tangled bulderbramble bushes. The soft soil surrenders to the weight of my feet, coating my footwear with a layer of grey dust. The vegetation on either side of me strokes my bare arms and legs. Occasionally a more solid branch prods me as I push my way through the undergrowth.

The further I follow Coell-J, the taller and denser the vegetation becomes. The thick branches scratch my flesh, drawing blood. The soil seems softer and wetter, making my progress more difficult. After a while I curse my curiosity and decide that I should turn around. My Secondary will doubtlessly note the dirt and blood on my clothes, even if my Primary doesn't. Questions will be asked. I might even be disciplined, or, worse, moved into a lower inculcation stratum. They've threatened me with as much before. I'll be destined to work in one of the Citadel factories or slaughterhouses.

I have to go back, I think.

But when I turn round, I see that both walkway and the Inculcatal Facility have disappeared behind the wall of plant-life, so I have no choice but to follow Coell-J, whose journey seems totally unimpeded by the vegetation. If anything, they're walking faster than before.

Should I call out to them? Beg them to take me back to the walkway I should never have strayed from in the first place, with the promise that I'll tell nobody that either of us were here? If they walk any faster, I might lose them altogether, which would be a disaster. I'm about to shout out to them when they stop. It's almost as though they heard me before I even spoke a word. Filled with a rush of gratitude, I push through the tangled foliage towards them. They're standing still, with their back to me, as if waiting. As I get closer, I notice that they've stopped in a small clearing; so small, in fact, that it could only comfortably accommodate one person. They still have their back to me, so I have no idea what they're doing.

A shiver of premonition runs through me. Only a few cycles ago I saw a Catharsis in which a Younger was slaughtered in the Broken Hemisphere. Is that what Coell-J intends for me? Their Designation unit is in the Outer Band, renowned for subversion. Criminality even. Is the quiet demeanour they affect in the Facility a façade that masks something darker?

My heart pounds. They move onwards, out of the clearing. I watch, with amazement, the branches and liptus grass curl inwards to fill the space in which Coell-J was standing. It's almost as though the vegetation moved aside to accommodate them. But that's not the end of it: as they walk forward, the plant-life in front of them gently bends to clear a pathway. Coell-J moves onwards, the green corridor closing behind them as they do.

Finally, they stop. With a sigh of leaf against leaf, Nature creates a larger area for our coming encounter, seeming to pause as the new boundary reaches my legs. Coell-J turns to face me. They smile. The grassy wall ripples around and behind me, larger leaves leaning inwards to form a canopy above us.

'Hello,' Coell-J says.

I'm not sure how to respond.

'Hello,' I eventually reply, then, gesturing towards the greenery, add, 'I didn't know that untethered Wildland could do that.'

'It can't,' they say, shaking their head but offering no further explanation.

If they intend to slaughter me, it doesn't show in their eyes, which are icily blue; something I've not noticed before. Their hands hang loosely at their side, fingers nervously toying with their crumpled linen shorts. Both their clothing and footwear are spotless, a stark contrast to mine, which are grubbier than they ever have been. Around their neck, on a thinly plaited chain of purple thread, hangs an odd-looking medallion.

'I heard you,' Coell-J states, sitting, their eyes still fixed on mine.

'I thought you must've done,' I say, copying them. As I sit, I brush against a particularly green tendril. Sap seeps onto my shorts. Another incriminating stain. 'I'm not as used to all this as you obviously are. I'm filthy, look! I must have tripped up at least four times. No wonder you heard me!'

'That's not what I meant,' Coell-J says enigmatically.

Again, they offer no explanation.

I'm starting to find their manner irritating. Regretting my inattention in the Anger Sublimation classes, I adopt my own method of emotional control, which I believe you would describe as 'distraction'. Like many things, the concept of distraction is so alien to our race that the word does not exist in my language. It implies that there is an alternative possibility to the path we are chosen for. And that is forbidden.

'Why aren't you dirty?' I demand. 'And what's that round your neck?'

Coell-J glances at my soiled clothing and bloodied arms and legs, then smiles again.

'This is a symbol of ancient fertility,' they reply calmly, pointing to a shape towards the bottom of the medallion.

'What's 'fertility?' I ask, then, when they don't reply, add, 'It's broken.'

'It's only a tiny crack,' they say, apparently indifferent to my criticism. 'I fell over at the Facility.'

They bow their head to survey the ground between us and choose a small gripp flower. Like the liptus grass that has woven itself into a wall around us, the flower is still alive but lying prostrate, splayed against the soil as if in surrender. Its petals are uneven, which intrigues me; the only gripp flowers I've seen before have been on the farms at the citadel's edge, meticulously arranged in precise, uniform rows with identical petals. Coell-J lifts their right hand, widens their fingers and holds it above the flower. Their blue eyes meet mine for an instant. I feel pierced by their icy intensity. After a second or two, they break the contact and look downwards.

I have absolutely no idea what is about to happen.

And yet…

I feel it first in my ears: the gentle rush of pressure building in the air around us. Silent to start with, but then the pressure gains a high-pitched voice, a whisper becoming a distant song. As the melody grows in size and volume, I feel the air prickle between us. This strange new electricity strokes my skin, fizzingly cold on my face, then it cascades away from me and down through Coell-J's fingers (which seem to be glowing, impossibly) and into the flower. Its petals ripple, leaves unfurl in the wave of energy and then, as if they're Players' puppets, the flower, grass and surrounding plant-life leap up and stand to attention, invigorated, seemingly more alive than they were before. The uneven petals gleam unnaturally.

Coell-J lowers their hand into their lap, admires the shining gripp flower for a moment, then smiles at me again.

'Did... did *you* do that?' I ask, incredulously.

They nod slowly. Something new in those icy blue eyes.

I look down at the gripp flower, whose iridescence is fading, then grab Coell-J's hands, both of them, turn them over, checking for wires. I've seen docu-casts about the trickery used in The Catharsae. But I can see no evidence of it here.

'How?!' I demand, abandoning Anger Sublimation and Distraction altogether. 'Tell me

14

how you did that, or I'll tell the inculcators that you broke the rules and came off the walkway!'

The smile vanishes. Coell-J's eyes harden.

My mouth becomes dry, anger giving way to fear. Then their expression softens; they're no longer my potential killer but a fellow Younger once again. I want to apologise for my empty threat, although I have the feeling that they already know they were in no danger from me. If I were to tell the inculcators that Coell-J had broken the law, I would also incriminate myself. Their face is kind; they mean me no harm.

They stand. I do too. Silently, we retrace our steps back towards the walkway. As we do so, the greenery parts for us and reforms behind us. This time, though, I know that it is doing so at Coell-J's bidding.

We part without words, because I have none.

4: Earth

Sunday 18th October, 2009

When Robert got to the graveyard, he realised just how long it had been since his previous visit. The gravestone was barely visible through the tangled mass of nettles, weeds and vines. There was no sign at all of the single red rose that he'd left on the first anniversary of James's death, though that was hardly a surprise. If any of the family had seen it, they would have immediately removed it, lest its meaning be inferred by passing acquaintances or fellow churchgoers. Robert shuddered at the bitter memory of being forcibly removed from the funeral, and Carol's dismay when her pleas on his behalf were met with cold disapproval. He'd begged her telepathically to let it be and she'd acquiesced eventually, though Robert was secretly pleased that she'd not done so quietly.

'Call yourself Christians? You should be ashamed of yourselves!'

He rather liked the way that Carol's righteous indignation always sounded like lines from an old TV drama. It was a quirk of character she shared with John and occasionally even Elena. Perhaps they inherited it from TIM, whose gentlemanly tones reminded Robert of a kindly deputy headmaster from *Grange Hill* or *Tom Brown's Schooldays*.

Although he knew they all meant well, Robert was sick of everyone treating him with kid gloves. Despite his complicated feelings about Paul, Robert missed his rebellious attitude to having to baby-sit the new arrival, or James's sulks when Robert challenged the incongruity of his believing in a deity that supposedly condemned their relationship. Neither Paul nor James patronised him. Neither were afraid of triggering one of his depressive periods, not that either of them ever could, because Robert felt validated by—and *present* with—them both.

But now Paul and James were gone. Like his parents. Like all his childhood friends. Stevie Cannon. Johnny Turner. Andy Cull. And for the moment at least, Robert was stuck here on Earth. Forbidden to use his powers in public. He felt hidden, different, pointless.

As he moved the stinging nettles aside, it occurred to Robert that James's family couldn't have been to the grave recently either. Maybe they'd been so sure that their gay son was burning in Hell that, after the public duty of the funeral, they'd abandoned all thought of him completely.

Robert felt the guttural tug of his loss sharper than ever before. *All* his losses; each painful separation reopening the healing wound of its predecessor. James's name glistened in silver, contrasting with the polished marble, the dates below it cruelly final, the memorial below them utterly meaningless. James Lanyon Kitto had not 'gone to sleep'. James

Lanyon Kitto was dead; he'd sacrificed himself in an act of humanity that none of his judgemental family would ever rival, or ever could. This was not James.

Robert?

His hands were erupting into painful nettle stings and his heart ached. But the tears would not come because in this state he was incapable of crying. He hadn't shed a single tear when his parents had been killed and that had been the danger sign that had led him to a child psychologist and ultimately into the medical facilities on the Trig.

Robert, where are you?

It was Paul who'd taught him how to shield his mind from the other Tomorrow People. Back then it had been a party trick, an act of mischief; typical Paul. Now it was a useful tool.

Robert needed to hide for a while before he made his final decision.

5: Barr-Byzhan

Dagre-Lunh, Sennith 0/ 1, Suncycle Thekh

The next time I see Coell-J at the Facility, they don't acknowledge me. The crystal blue eyes are lowered, apparently indifferent; in fact, there is no communication of any sort between us for several senniths. I start to wonder whether I've imagined the whole unlikely business in the Wildland; neither my Primary nor my Secondary admonished me for the state of my clothing or skin, after all. And when I return to the point on the walkway where we entered the Wildland, there is no sign that the vegetation has been disturbed.

Did it actually happen?

The answer is presented to me when Coell-J finally acknowledges me, on the same walkway. Though no words pass between us, I know they're going to step off into the Wildland at any moment. Sure enough, the grasses part, inviting both of us in.

The experience is exactly the same as the first time, and then Coell-J reaches out and takes hold of my left hand. Their fingers are warm and slightly clammy to the touch.

'Try it,' they say, withdrawing their hand from mine.

'How?' I ask, feeling faintly ridiculous.

The gripp flower stands patiently below my outstretched hand, awaiting my command. Coell-J smirks lightly. There's the tiniest ripple of its leaves in reply. I suddenly realise how absurd I'm being, endowing vegetation with sentient thought, as if it were alive and—

Ready.

Coell-J's word finishes my thought. But it isn't. Coell-J said nothing. They're sitting in silence, patiently observing. They seem to genuinely believe that I can make the flower move, like they did, without any knowledge of the trickery involved. The gripp flower shivers. I feel the lightest tingle in my fingertips, an echo of the energy of a few moments ago. Coell-J senses it, nods supportively.

Focus, the flower says.

In Coell-J's voice.

The vibration moves from my fingertips to the centre of my hand, and I become aware of the same distant rush. Then the whisper. Then the song. But this time it's different. This time I can *taste* the air as it cools between us, then flows into me. I can *smell* it trickling down my throat, feel it progress through my blood and muscles and into my fingers, which are glowing, just as Coell-J's did, a gleaming blue light.

It's new. Terrifying. Exhilarating.

Now, ask, the flower says.

I ask the flower to lie down. But say no words. It quivers, sighs, sending a ripple of movement out into the liptus grass, into the surrounding air, and I begin to understand. We are connected, the gripp flower, the vegetation, the soil, myself. I ask again. And now *everything* is iridescent, filled with shades of blue and white that I've never noticed before, perhaps never known.

The flower smiles and lies down, singing.

Then Coell-J places their hand on top of mine and says, with no words, the whole of it. Their fingers are glowing, the whispering energy is gathering around us, coalescing, brushing our skin before it enters us.

Us.

Our hands seem to blend into one. I can feel their pulse, blood pumping faster and faster as the shining energy envelops us. And now I smell their memories, taste their last meal, the salt of tears on their cheek and on their lips as each mooncycle of their life ends and begins again. I'm surfing now on the wave of time that rips through their suncycles and we are the same.

Concentrate! I feel them urge, *the plantlife!*

I fall into the present moment, into the shining ball of light that our hands have become. I see our life force crackle into the flower, creating a web-like pattern of energy that grows, spreads into the stem and into the leaves and into the ground, snaking into every blade of liptus grass and every fragment of soil beneath us. There's no need for us to ask the greenery to lie down for us now, because we are at one with it; it knows what we need it to do. The gripp flower at the centre of Us shudders, then gifts us its pollen: thousands of microscopic grains dancing into our skin, singing in our veins. Trees and branches at the edge of our glade shake then bend backwards as our light touches them and, plant by plant, tree by tree, the vegetation tumbles downwards, a shockwave spreading outwards, ever faster, until the whole of the Wildland is flattened. We are naked to the outside world now, two Youngers, hand in hand, heads bowed together, blazing with blue light.

The moment the image occurs to me, Coell-J gasps, pulls their hand away, and the connection ends. The plantlife snaps back into place, the light fades.

Our glade, comfortably spacious before, is a lot smaller now. Branches obscure my view of Coell-J. The air is damp and chilled. For the first time I'm aware of the mechanical thrum of the city and traffic beyond the greenery. It seems intrusive, alien.

'We can't do this again,' Coell-J mutters from behind the leafy barrier. 'If we were seen...'

'Do you think we were?'

I feel panic rising. I notice that my fingernails are stained with pollen.

'I don't think so,' Coell-J reassures me, 'but if we *had* been... They might think we're Nikeys.'

I've heard the word before, without really understanding its meaning, other than it being an insult. A word reserved for Youngers who are excused from the more taxing Sublimation Exercises for 'health reasons'. Once I saw a weeping Younger surrounded by a circle of taunting crueltors, chanting 'Nikey!' The inculcator on duty did nothing to stop the attack, which shocked me to the core: not only is the act of openly weeping forbidden, the crueltors were brazenly disobeying the strictly enforced Rule of Silence in areas outside the Inculcatal Halls. The crueltored Younger was removed from the Upper Stratum soon afterwards; I've not seen them since. A couple of senniths later I saw a Catharsis in which a Not Like was treated in the same way by a group of normal Citizens, and I laughed along with everyone else.

Even now I fail to see the connection between the nickname and the Not Like. Nor do I understand how the astonishing experience that I've just had could relate to either. All I know is that what we've done is abnormal. Unnatural.

Wrong.

I mention it to no-one. Despite Coell-J's reservations, we do indulge in the ritual from time to time afterwards, but only when we are certain not to be observed. None of the other Youngers know that we have exchanged anything more than a cursory greeting. When Coell-J is absent from the Facility for more than a sennith, rumours start circling that they've been sent to a Readjustment Institution. Barram-N, the Upper Stratum's highest achiever, tells us that their Primary Designator has indisputable proof that Coell-J is Not Like. When asked what the 'indisputable proof' is, they have no answers.

With Coell-J gone, I can concentrate fully on my Sublimation & Inculcation Programme. My ratings have slipped considerably since that first time in the Wildland. Focussing on standard exercises and levels of achievement, I fool myself into believing that I can become a Citizen in the way that my Designators intend, that I am healthily normal, and that the Wildland was a passing aberration. My ratings improve. My Designators are pleased, though they know better than to demonstrate their pride at any more than the acceptable level.

For a while I excel. But it is all a lie.

It is during this time that I first hear your voice.

6: Earth

Having made his decision, Robert bade farewell to James's grave and made his way back to the church. He could have walked to Barcombe Hill—it would have taken a couple of hours at the most—but the longer he stayed away from the Lab, the more likely it would be that TIM would track him down on CCTV, or Carol would succeed in breaking through his psychic shield. Of course, there was a strong possibility that they would locate him when he used his jaunting belt (that was why he'd hidden it in the first place) but by then he'd be where he wanted to be anyway, so it wouldn't really matter.

Robert needed to return to a time before he broke out, a time before Jedikiah, the Lab, the Trig, a time when everything was uncomplicated, when he, Johnny, Stevie and Andy had the whole of the South Downs to play *Doctor Who* or *Indiana Jones* on, endless summer holidays to waste and no responsibilities at all. Short of persuading the Guardians of Time to let him actually return, jaunting back to Barcombe Hill seemed the closest he could get to it.

A pipe dream, of course. The village had changed almost beyond recognition even in the few years he'd been living there. And he knew that his childhood hadn't really been that idyllic. Growing up with grandparents too old and tired to offer anything more than rudimentary care wasn't easy, and his friendship group had fallen apart as soon as Andy had disappeared and Robert had been taken into psychiatric care.

The church was cool and hissingly silent. It took a few moments for Robert's eyes to adjust to the change in light. But soon the gaudy, blinding colours of the stained glass mellowed. Patterns in the stonework surrounding the windows emerged from the darkness: rivers of smooth mortar sloshing around uneven stones, like mountain ranges viewed from the sky. Robert remembered the tranquil hours he'd spent with Andy, laying on damp grass up at the Devil's Hoof, studying the surface of every standing stone in the circle. The whole village believed it had been built in the bronze age, until John, Elena and Paul discovered the truth: it was a distress beacon built by aliens. Of course.

Whether it was alien or not, the circle certainly emitted power, and Robert had felt it. Just as he felt a presence here, now, in the church. There was no physical manifestation, at least not yet. The weathered wooden pews were empty, hopeful home-stitched hassocks lined up in readiness for God-fearing knees on Sunday. An ugly modern organ, square pipes grey and bland, was locked and muted. A Bible, its worn leather cracked, sat patiently open on a functional wooden lectern in front of a neat, unpretentious altar. Somewhere, distantly, a sparrow chirruped, to no response.

Yet Robert felt its presence. *His* presence. His skin was tingling with it. The blood began to rumble in his ears as his heart pounded in the same way that it had, over two years ago, when he first met…

James?

Robert's vision blurred. There was a pain in his abdomen; he was overcome by nausea. He glanced to his left and saw… *someone*. A passing shadow, moving up the aisle. There but not there. A ghost?

James, is that you?

The figure stopped a foot away from the altar, facing away from Robert. He knew him. *He knew him.*

'James?'

Robert was crying now.

The figure turned.

'Robert?!'

Andy. It was Andy Cull. Older now, taller, with prematurely grey hair, wearing torn combat fatigues and muddy boots. Holding a large gold-plated candlestick in one hand and Robert's jaunting belt in the other.

'What the hell are you doing here?'

A sudden burst of energy roared past Robert's head and hit Andy squarely in the chest. His eyes widened then closed as he crumpled to the floor. A masked figure strode past Robert, leant over his unconscious friend and retrieved the belt. Then, turning round, they removed their mask and hat.

'Are you all right, Robert? We've been worried about you.'

A second wave of pain ripped through him. The hammering in his ears blocked out her words, his vision disappeared completely, and he fell to his knees, sobbing.

7: Barr-Byzhan

Dagre-Hermh, Sennith 1/ 4, Suncycle Triah

I hear your voice, but I don't recognise it for what it is. I dismiss it as a dream, albeit a waking one. You say no words; maybe there *are* no words for what you are feeling or for what we are sharing, without realising it.

It is not unusual for me to be distracted from my studies, whether by a waking dream or by the contemplation of a world that exists outside the Inculcatal Facility. At the time when other Youngers are forging the inculcatal paths that will unite them with their pairbonders, I prefer to be alone, sketching imaginary scenes from the *Lost Shrine of the Ancients* (my favourite vidcast) or daydreaming about the Wildland.

The cruelty comes from nowhere. It starts with barely concealed whispers, taunts which become insulting notes left at my workbench. Before long I have to endure the mocking circle I saw before, and the crueltors, once more unchallenged by the Inculcator on duty, use the same language. For daring to be something other than the norm, I am a 'Nikey'.

I don't tell my Designators. My studies suffer. Soon I have been moved from the Upper Stratum into the Lower, where I belong.

Out in the world beyond the Facility, Hatch-G-Mah is about to launch a moral crusade that will win them the Establishmentorship (over our hemisphere at least) but as a Younger I have no interest in politics, and no comprehension that they might have any effect on my life. A news story has recently broken about Thorrus-J-Remm, one of Hatch-G-Mah's most powerful rivals, the one most likely to

29

defeat them in the race for Establishmentorship. Evidence has come to light that Thorrus-J-Remm is Not Like. I'm pretending to be working on an assignment when the vidcast moves on to their story, promising coverage of the latest damning evidence. My Secondary strides across the living pod, grabs the vid-control and flicks it off.

'We don't want to see any of *that* nonsense, thank you very much!' they snap.

The following sennith, Thorrus-J-Remm is banished to the Broken Hemisphere and Hatch-G-Mah delivers the speech that will seal their victory as Establishmentor:

'Our most important task in this Establishmentorship will be to raise the quality of Personal Inculcation. It's in the planetary interest. And it's in the individual interest of every Designator and above all, of every Younger. We want inculcation to be part of the answer to our world's problems, not part of the cause. Too often, our Youngers don't get the inculcation they need—the inculcation they deserve. Here, in the Outer Band of this very citadel—where Youngers must have decent inculcation if they are to have a better future; that opportunity is all too often snatched from them by dissident inculcation authorities and extremist inculcators. Youngers who need to be able to express themselves in clear Barr-Byzhian are being taught political slogans. Youngers who need to be taught to respect traditional moral values are being taught that they have an inalienable right to be Not Like. All of those Youngers are being cheated of a sound start in life—yes, cheated!'

Soon after Establishmentor Hatch's landslide election, my Primary calls me into their workspace, so I know it must be something serious. I've only ever been allowed in there a handful of times, and then it's only been a brief visit: a palmprint to accompany a Learning Application or a vidcall with the Head of Facility when I was lower-stratumed. They close the door and invite me to sit down. Whatever they have to say is not for the ears of my Secondary. I'm suddenly frozen with fear that somehow my Primary has found out what I did in the Wildland and that they're going to send me to the Readjustment Institution to rot with Coell-J and the other perverteds.

I study the floor, unable to meet my Primary's eyes.

'Daghu-N,' they say slowly, sitting in the large, well-worn chair on the other side of their neatly organised workbench, 'your Secondary and I have been talking about your ratings since you were reassigned to a less taxing stratum…'

So that's all it is: inculcatal work. I'm relieved, morbid fantasies of running away to the Broken Hemisphere receding.

'They're average,' they continue, 'which is acceptable. What *isn't* acceptable is that you've yet to choose a pairbonder.'

This is surprising.

'It's not abnormal for you not to have made a firm decision at your age,' they admit, rather awkwardly, standing to pace the chamber. 'but we might have expected you to have at least shown an interest…'

'I *am* interested!' I protest.

My Primary looks over at me, raising an eyebrow.

'Barram-L,' I announce, plucking a name out of the air.

My Primary frowns.

'Barram-N,' they say, 'Wasn't that the Top-grader of your last stratum? I hardly think…'

'Not Barram-N,' I correct them, 'Barram-L.'

Barram-L is N's younger sibling and one of the few not to tease me about my self-inflicted solitude.

'Barram,' my Primary repeats thoughtfully, then wanders over to their info screen and types in the name.

The screen flickers into life, displaying genetic information, achievement statistics and so on, all of which seems to please my Primary.

'Barram-L's Primary Designator has a leading role in the Council of West Pyramids,' they comment. 'That's excellent. Well, Daghu-N, I'd say you made a wise choice there. As to whether you'd better suit Primary or Secondary… but we mustn't get ahead of ourselves, there's still time to choose. I'm not sure whether the West Pyramids have choice regulations, we'll have to check. Excellent.'

And these are the last words that my Primary and I exchange about pairbonding. Any further discussion (which is minimal) is charged to my Secondary.

It's a while before I dare to share the conversation with Barram-L. Before I do, I endeavour to spend more time with them, usually at a Catharsis or in one of our living pods. This at least gives the impression that we are contemplating a future together. My Designators leave us to it, and a potential connection with the West Pyramids dynasty seems enough for them to abandon their pestering me with suggestions that I strive for higher grades at the Facility. When I finally broach the subject of pairbonding with Barram-L, they are appalled,

33

which I find first perplexing and then hurtful. Later, of course, I understand that their reaction is less to do with me and more with the West Pyramids' perception of those born into a lesser stratum of society.

The Daghus are not good enough for the Barrams, it would seem.

8: Earth

Monday 19th October, 2009

'There's nothing wrong with me—I fainted, that's all!'

'Keep still, Robert, we're nearly finished.'

Robert lowered his head back onto the plastic examination bed with a sigh. The fizzing scanner beams continued their progress up his body, a series of irritating beeps matching the lights that pulsed across one of TIM's spheres. Then, as the scan reached the top of his forehead, the beeping and flashing stopped, and the only sounds were the air-conditioning and the gentle throb of power cells. Although the tubes and wires that connected the cells to TIM's main body on the ceiling would have looked retro—archaic—to Robert's contemporaries, he knew that behind the clunky façade lay one of the most advanced pieces of machinery ever installed on Earth. In the wrong hands, TIM, the ultimate in Artificial Intelligence hardware, would be virtually unbeatable as a Weapon of Mass Destruction, even in the slightly under par state his systems were in after a Tnawi virus had attacked all of the Federation's hardware. And here he was, being used to conduct an MRI scan on a perfectly healthy young man! Robert's grandfather would have been appalled at the scandalous waste of resources; he'd been apoplectic when the Barcombe and Area Council squandered funds on a 'completely unnecessary' car park up on Devil's Hoof and fought plans to develop the village's derelict theatre into a leisure facility until his dying day.

'Well, TIM?' Carol asked, looking up at the softly glowing spheres (a meaningless old habit she couldn't shake off; if she wanted to communicate facially with TIM she'd have been better off addressing one of the walls, which were invisibly full of sensors).

'Apart from slightly raised adrenalin levels,' TIM replied, his spheres flashing in time with the answer, 'Robert's physiology is completely normal.'

'Told you!' Robert snapped, sitting up and flipping himself into a standing position.

'Just a moment,' Carol laid a gentle but restraining hand on his arm. 'That's good news, but what were you thinking of, taking off your jaunting belt? *And* powering it down? What if something had happened to you? If that boy hadn't switched it on, we'd never have found you...'

'But nothing *is* going to happen to me, is it?' Robert grumbled. 'Not down here. Not while we're hiding underground like... like moles!'

'Oh Robert,' Carol smiled fondly, 'it's not that bad. And I can assure you, it's no more interesting up there on the Trig! You heard what Elena said yesterday—if she has to check one more data diagnostic, she'll scream!'

'It's not just that,' said Robert, 'it's... oh I don't know. None of it seems... fair. We saved them—we *saved the world*—and none of the Saps know it!'

'None of them must *ever* know it, Robert,' said TIM sternly.

Carol nodded.

'TIM's right,' she affirmed. 'You know how paranoid the Saps are now; how fragile the world is at the moment. That boy in the church—a Scavenger gang member by the look of it—what if he'd had a knife? A gun?'

'He wouldn't have used it.'

36

'You don't know that, Robert!'

'I do,' Robert replied, sitting down deflatedly. 'I know him. *Knew* him. Andy Cull. We grew up together, about ten miles away from where you found me. He'd never harm me.'

Carol sat next to him and gazed at one of the pulsating walls for a moment before saying:

'I'm afraid he might have done, if he'd known who... *what* you are. It's a different world now. They're terrified of anything, anyone that's different from them. To them, we're the same as the Tnawi. We're the enemy.'

9: Barr-Byzhan

Dagre-Lunh, Sennith 0/1, Suncycle Teshr

Despite every attempt to distract myself, to believe that the experiences in the Wildland were a passing aberration, I find myself curious to repeat them. However, thanks to Establishmentor Hatch's insistent moral orations on the vidcasts, I am increasingly certain that what I felt there was wrong.

After their initial dismissal, Barram-L seems to have a change of heart about pairbonding. Much to the concern of Barram-L's Designators and to the delight of mine, we spend even more time together. The crueltors lose interest in me. Without knowing it, Barram-L is acting as the perfect smokescreen for what I'm slowly becoming. Then, almost three suncycles after the Wildland experiences, things change.

On New Cycle's Day, Barram-L's Designators are to host a Second Naming Ceremony to celebrate their eldest's Validation. It is a rite of passage that, to the rest of us, is marked with a Designation unit meal, followed by the signing of deeds that give us both our third name and official recognition as a valid Byzhan Citizen. The East and West Pyramids celebrate the passing from Younger to Citizen with considerably more style, of course. Barram-N, having consistently been the highest achiever in the Upper Stratum, has a secure pairbonding with another high achiever. They're also certain to be Primary Designator once the bonding has taken place. They are the model Byzhan, their perfectly balanced facial features and efficacious physique ensuring that they will live a long and productive life at the heart of the West Pyramid elite. In their less guarded moments, Barram-L has been scathing of N's apparent perfection, but custom dictates that they are to present their sibling with the validation gown and pledge their allegiance before an audience of distinguished elders. There is a rumour that Establishmentor Hatch themself might even be in attendance, so I confess to being secretly pleased when I am invited to the ceremony.

My Secondary can barely contain their delight at the prospect, until my Primary reminds them that such a reaction betrays our social stratum and warns me to outwardly curb any enthusiasm I might feel.

'In times to come,' they state calmly, alluding to my imminent pairbonding, 'attending these events will become second nature to you.'

Four senniths later. as we approach the Temple of the West Pyramids, I find that difficult to believe.

10: Earth

Thursday 22nd October, 2009

KEEP OUT. THIS AREA HAS BEEN DECLARED GEOLOGICALLY UNSAFE BY THE WORLD GOVERNMENT. DANGER OF DEATH.

The sign, though dated by mention of the World Government, looked brand-new, gleaming in the autumnal sunshine with no sign of decay, unlike the huge, rusting fence it was attached to.

Beneath the lettering was a bold logo that Robert didn't recognise. If it was supposed to be lettering, it was badly designed, probably by committee. E.D.O.S. perhaps? European Department of Safety? Whichever company it belonged to, they'd made a thorough job of cutting Barcombe Hill off from the outside world; the fence must be at least twelve feet tall and seemed to surround the entire village. Looking up towards the Downs, he could tell that even the Devil's Hoof had been declared 'geologically unsafe'. Perhaps it had become so when Caine and her department had removed the spaceship from its resting place beneath the stone circle? They would have had little concern for preserving the hole left behind once they'd removed their precious cargo.

Flicking the power switch of his jaunting belt to standby, Robert waited for a telepathic chastisement from TIM or Carol, but none came. It seemed that leaving the Lab during the daily communication from the Trig had paid off.

He gazed thoughtfully through the fence at the abandoned village, wondering where he could jaunt across to safely, without the belt's precision, or not being spotted—if there was anyone to spot him. The green seemed too open, even if he managed to materialise behind a tree, the churchyard too cluttered with greenery. A side road, maybe, or the car park next to the pub? Robert frowned. The pub seemed different. A change of colour perhaps? New landlords determined to put their stamp on their purchase with a lick of paint? The locals wouldn't have taken much notice; the pub was the pub was the pub. And as long as it stocked the same local ales and hosted the weekly quiz in the Devil's Nook bar... *That was it.* He could see the Devil's Nook from here, so-called because, according to legend, Satan liked to have a pint on the Winter's Solstice, daringly hidden in plain sight only feet away from St Mary's... which wasn't there. Which was why Robert could see the Devil's Nook from this angle.

The whole church had disappeared.

In its place, he now realised, was an uneven stretch of wasteland, a mess of vegetation, soil and rocks that could well be the broken remains of St Mary's. Had a rogue Tnawi missile destroyed it, or was this a result of the geological fault referred to on the signs?

Something darted between two of the large pieces of rock at the far end of the wasteland. An animal? Robert waited for further movement, but he saw none. Then there was a quick flash from the pub as an opening door reflected the sunlight. A young man in combat fatigues appeared briefly in the doorway, quickly retreating back into the shadows. Another movement from the wasteland: not an animal after all, but a similarly clad figure. One of the Scavenger gangs was obviously using the Devil's Nook as a base. The thump of body against earth was followed by a guttural cry, which itself was succeeded by the grumbling rush of smaller stones. The runner had fallen to the ground, which bizarrely seemed to be moving beneath them.

'Johnny!'

The cry was hoarse and desperate. The other man reappeared in the pub doorway as rocks started to roll across the ground towards the fallen one. Robert jaunted, just in time to see Stevie Cannon being swallowed up by swirling gravel.

'Get away from there!' the man shouted from the Devil's Nook.

He was bearded, gaunt, old before his time, but recognisably Johnny Turner. Robert opened his mouth to reply but no words came. The ground disappeared beneath him, and he fell, a sharp boulder hitting the back of his head as he did.

11: Barr-Byzhan

A massive structure towering over the city, the Temple of the West Pyramids' gold-encrusted twin turrets seem to pierce the clouds, gleaming in the sunlight like two flaming torches. A huge, ornately patterned window glistens like a rippling lake between them, giving the impression that the whole building is alight and swaying in the breeze.

There are hundreds of us, all walking in perfect unison, all silent and all dressed in identical white robes. Mine belonged to my Primary and has had to be carefully altered to fit me. Barram-L's is brand new and will probably only be worn once, a sign of the West Pyramids' affluence.

The Ceremonial Chamber is high-ceilinged, an exquisitely painted arched roof supported by large pillars crafted from polished blackstone. The grand window looks even more impressive from the inside, its riot of colours exploding onto the walls, the blackstone reflecting the flames of a hundred candles, each lit by clerics in hourly rituals during the preceding sennith. Two gigantic doors dominate the wall opposite the window. They're ornately carved, a series of freezes depicting the Ancient

43

Prophets' arrival on Barr-Byzhan and their ensuing domination over both hemispheres. The firelight and shimmering colours pick out different details at random, giving the impression that the whole chamber is a living entity. In front of the doors there is a large platform, festooned with the standards of the West and East Pyramids. On the platform are eight thrones and a lectern crafted from the same polished blackstone as the pillars. At the foot of the lectern, carved out of the same piece of stone, sit two hefty hunting birds, territorially facing outwards. For a moment I think they're alive, their beaks clucking in disapproval at the ostentatiousness of it all, until I realise that the sound is coming from branches slapping against lower windows on either side of the platform—the temple has been built on a section of Wildland, dominating it as if to prove the Byzhans' mastery.

We process down the long central aisle of the chamber, past a grand, polished display case filled with gleaming holy artefacts and take our places near the platform. I am surprised to be seated next to Barram-L, but, wary of my Primary's advice, show nothing. I know that neither Barram-L nor Barram-N have been allowed into this part of the Temple before. Both seem indifferent to its opulence, although I am sure one thing can't have escaped their notice.

It's just like the Lost Shrine of the Ancients!

Although, at first, I assume that the whisper came from Barram-L, their head is lowered in supplication.

The doors are exactly the same!

The voice comes from behind us and belongs to Barram-N, or Barram-N-Coll as he will be addressed henceforth. I turn to nod in agreement, but the seats behind us are empty. The line of attendees are waiting patiently at the main entrance to the chamber, as Establishmentor Hatch takes their place at the head of the primary procession. Standing beside them, customarily naked and holding a white bundle of ceremonial robes in front of their waist, is Barram-N-Coll, staring first at the impressive doors... and then directly at me.

The wind is bellowing outside, battering against the twin towers and making every pane of stained-glass rattle. Barram-N-Coll's Designators and pairbonder elect take their places behind the Establishmentor and N-Coll, whose eyes are now fixed firmly on the platform ahead. Their skin is pale, almost translucent. At their groin are the beginnings of the primary genitalia, so their role must have been designated, the necessary medical treatment begun.

As the ceremonial anthem starts, an especially strong gust of wind roars around the towers. The infrastructure yawns under the pressure, its metal struts, blackened with age, groaning a tuneless bass line to the high-pitched voices of the choir. The procession shuffles forward. Barram-L stands and takes their place in the aisle, ready to receive the ceremonial robes from their sibling. Establishmentor Hatch acknowledges none of us as they sweep past and up onto the platform, where they sit in one of the thrones reserves for dignitaries and high clerics. Barram-L takes the robes from N-Coll, glancing at the forming genitalia, the lightest mockery playing on their lips. Their Primary sees the disrespect and flashes a look of disapproval. Barram-L blushes and steps back as their sibling leads the main participants up the steps and onto the platform. As soon as Barram-N-Coll is kneeling, head bowed in supplication to the quaking window, the massive wooden doors swing open and the anthem ends.

A grandly attired cleric steps forward into the chamber, slowly mounting the platform. I recognise the face immediately: it belongs to Their Holiness the Commander of Clerics. Quite a coup for the Barrams and the West Pyramids! Their Holiness is accompanied by similarly uniformed representatives from the various clerical orders, each taking a place on the platform. The only sounds are their footsteps, the wind and the branches slapping on the lower windows. The Commander of Clerics stands at the lectern, their gold-embroidered gown's design echoing the hunting birds at its base. These birds are less sedate than the blackstone pair, claws raised in attack, eyes fiery and vengeful rather than silently judgemental. Could these be the Twin Fowls of the Sublimation, the creatures that inspired the First Prophet to suppress all unnecessary emotions in the first place, to achieve the State of Grace to which all Byzhans aspire? If so, their representation is more lively than one might have expected; the two birds of legend were mute beasts that barely stirred over the many suncycles of their long lives.

Later I will understand that this is typical of the many paradoxes that exist within the Clericdom, whose iron hold over the Establishment (and thus over us all) is corrupt and unbreakable.

Their Holiness greets the Establishmentor with a brief nod of the head and then consults a heavy, antiquated book before addressing the congregation:

'In the name of The Creator, I call upon you all to bow your heads in shame, as befits all those who are imperfect and live under the Sacred Sword of Judgement…'

All heads are lowered, except for those of Establishmentor Hatch, whose mind would appear to be on other matters, and Barram-N-Coll, whose eyes are once again burning into mine. I feel my face redden and lower my head. The branches slapping on the windows seems to intensify.

'Spare us, O Creator, from the chaos of untethered emotion. Free us from the weakness of our ancestors, who stumbled in the darkness before you granted us Light to guide us…'

Slap. Slap.

'Accept our contriteness as we offer our finest Younger to your Citizenship and service, in the certainty that they will strive for the State of Grace…'

Slap. Slap. Slap.

The wind is growing stronger now. And there's something else. Something achingly familiar.

'In accepting our gift, O Creator, allow us to raise our eyes to your realm, that we might…'

The Commander of Clerics stops mid-sentence. I know before I raise my eyes what they have seen, because I've heard the whispering, I've tasted the coldness in the air... Barram-N-Coll's naked body is shining with blue light. It's streaming outwards from them and filling every crack in the ancient floor, pulling the untamed Wildland towards them.

Help me!

I hear their voice as clearly as the roaring wind above us. I feel their hands on my shoulders, smell their fear, taste their breath, even though a crowd of lesser clerics, moving forward to protect Their Holiness, are now obscuring my view of N-Coll.

The wind's roar increases. The Commander of Clerics is dumbfounded. Establishmentor Hatch looks appalled. The branches are hammering against the windows now. Citizen Barram stands, shouts, 'Who is responsible for this?!' The whole temple is shuddering now. N-Coll's Secondary looks terrified.

The lower windows shatter. Establishmentor Hatch strides off the platform and down the aisle, where a contingent of armed guards surround them, ready to protect their leader. The Commander of Clerics raises their hands as if to implore The Creator to bring an end to this madness.

Barram-N-Coll falls to the floor,

The blue light fades.

The storm passes.

Barram-L rushes towards the platform and covers their sibling with the ceremonial robes, clutching them, face contorted with concern. N-Coll's pairbonder elect hasn't moved. They sit in their throne, watching the scene impassively, the model student.

I say nothing. But my mind is racing.

12: Earth

Thursday 22nd October, 2009

Robert opened his eyes, unsure whether it was the blood rushing in his ears that had woken him or... something else. The tunnel was only dimly illuminated by distant daylight; he'd fallen quite some way, it seemed. A nagging ache in his side intimated a collision with one of the rocks punctuating the shaft he'd fallen down. The tired groan of metal occasionally cut across a constant gurgle of water splashing against rock. A stream? Robert couldn't tell. He struggled onto his elbows and immediately regretted it. A sharp pain seared across the back of his head. He brought his hand up to its source; the wound was open, his neck soaked with blood.

There was a sudden sound to his right, very close. Something guttural: an animal? It was breathing, growling, in pain maybe. Robert, dizzy with panic and the loss of blood, reached out along the ground beside him, found something sharp and metal and picked it up. With the other hand, he flipped the switch on his jaunting belt, which hummed into life.

'Stevie?!'

Johnny Turner's voice echoed down the shaft. Shards of light pierced the darkness, search beams illuminating the bloodied face of Robert's old friend, skin yellowing with decay, dead eyes staring, his mouth hanging open in a silent scream. Halfway up Stevie's body, a scrawny creature looked up from its meal, squatting on thick thighs, hungry eyes glistening in the torchlight. A firm crocodile-like jaw protruded from the top of its long neck, teeth menacingly sharp. Its body was ape-like, its arms thin with long, claw-like fingers. A shabby tail stood on end, like a cat's when it's sensing danger.

The belt emitted a calm, resolute bleep. Robert pressed the central button at the exact moment that the creature leapt towards him.

13: Barr-Byzhan

An investigation ensues into who tried to sabotage Barram-N-Coll's Second Naming Ceremony and, though no accusations or arrests are made in the first few senniths, the general opinion is that it was a political act. It was, after all, Hatch-G-Mah's first official ceremonial visitation as Establishmentor and the eyes of Barr-Byzhan were on the temple. If the culprits could fool the world into believing that the Top-grader that the Establishmentor so publicly supported was—let's not mince words here—a Not Like, then their moral high ground might be perceived to rest on unstable foundations. Blame settles eventually on the Outer Island Radicals, a group of terrorists, perverteds that publicly condemned Thorrus-J-Remm's arrest and banishment. Vidcasts soon emerge of a well-orchestrated raid on a political meeting in the Broken Hemisphere, at which Thorrus-J-Remm is speaking. The disgraced politician, already banished, is arrested and imprisoned, as are all the attendees. The Outer Island Radicals' voice is silenced forever.

Establishmentor Hatch's moral standing remains firm, their leadership stronger and Barram-N-

Coll's pairbonding service is brought forward, their innocence in the whole affair unquestioned.

But I know better. Barram-N-Coll was controlling the Wildland outside the temple in the same way that Coell-J and I once did. And for some reason I was able to see into their mind, to hear their voice; for a moment we were connected. Which means they are like me.

And we are Not Like.

Six senniths after the ceremony I attempt to contrive a situation where Barram-N-Coll and I can be alone together. Their pairbonding would seem to provide the perfect alibi: as preparations gather apace, it is customary for the extended Designation units to arrange a series of feasts to which I, as Barram-L's pairbonder elect, am invited, although I know by now that I will never pairbond with Barram-L. The Not Like do not pairbond—it is a prisonable offence.

The Feast is as dull as might be expected, the conversation occasional and lacklustre. To my disappointment, Barram-N-Coll neither greets me nor makes eye contact at all whilst we're eating. They respond to every comment I make with silence. Even when the subject of their Second Naming Ceremony is brought up, N-Coll shows no sign of remembering the moment we shared. Far from it. They speak of the imprisoned perverteds with utter contempt. As the participants leave, I pretend to be adjusting a faulty bootlace, knowing that custom demands that N-Coll must be the last to leave the table.

At last we are alone.

N-Coll is seated still, apparently contemplating their pale, unblemished hands on the table in front of them.

'N-Coll…' I begin.

They raise their head to look at me for the first time. Their fury chills me.

'I know it was you!' they spit accusingly, all proprietary having vanished. 'I felt it. If it weren't for Barram-L, I'd have had you arrested and thrown into prison with those other perverteds! I hope for your sake and Barram-L's that you turn yourself in to the correctional authorities before it's too late. It's a disease. Get help. And I don't want you at my pairbonding service. Feign ill health. Anything, I don't care. Now get out.'

I feel betrayed, baffled, dirty.

Then comes the Madness.

14: Earth

'First Andy, then Stevie and Johnny. It's mad! I mean that has to be more than a coincidence, doesn't it?'

Robert was alone again and hurting and wanted someone to talk to, and that someone wasn't a well-meaning older woman from the Galactic Federation or a biotronic computer hanging from a ceiling somewhere below London; that someone was James. But James didn't reply because James was dead. Stevie was dead. His parents were dead. His grandparents too. But if James had been right, their spirits lived on. And his grave would be a logical meeting place—if there was such a thing—between the spirit world and the corporeal one. So, if there was the remotest chance… Oh, who was he kidding?

'You'd say it was God's will, I suppose,' he continued, his head throbbing. He'd stopped bleeding now, but he probably needed to go to hospital, or be checked out by TIM at the very least. But not yet. 'Divine providence or something. Very kind of your merciful God to let me see one of my schoolfriends being eaten by an alien!'

He stroked the twisted piece of metal that had wounded him: another KEEP OUT sign, whose ragged edge punished his finger with a sharp slice. So sharp, in fact, that it took a few seconds for the cut to bleed. Robert winced.

'Sorry. You hated it when I said that kind of thing, didn't you? Got to admit it; I sometimes said things to provoke a heated debate. You were so cute when you got up on your soapbox, hun.'

Hun. Babes. Sweetie. James had hated all that too, especially in public, or in front of the other TPs. Public displays of affection were definitely out of bounds; their affair had been conducted behind closed doors, furtive moments of passion grasped when nobody was looking, even in the UC1 machine. It had driven Robert to distraction back then. Now he'd settle for the chastest of hugs.

'John always told me there was no such thing as a coincidence, that everything had a rational explanation if you looked hard enough. I suppose it's true. It's no coincidence that I'm back here, is it? The belt locked on to one of its last safe set of co-ordinates. And it makes sense that Johnny and Stevie would be hiding out in Barcombe Hill. Maybe Andy is there as well, and just happened to be scavenging here when I bumped into him—it's not far. God, I feel sick…'

He watched his blood drip onto the rose in front of the gravestone, ruby red on garish yellow.

'I wish you weren't bloody dead, James.'

Red on yellow.

He felt the bile rise in his throat as he remembered the tortured expression on Stevie's yellowing face. He thought of all the death he'd witnessed since he'd been drawn into the world of Homo Superior. All the final moments he'd witnessed, all the bodies he'd seen decaying.

No. That wasn't right.

Stevie's body hadn't had time to decay. He'd been alive when he fell into the tunnel.

And there was something else... something obvious... Red on yellow...

Robert's skin tingled, his vision blurred. Someone was here. Close.

Who are you? I know you're here; I can feel you. James, is it you? Please, let it be you. I want you to be right. I want your spirit to have survived. Please, let it be you... Please...

Carol saw Robert pass out as she hurried out of the church. Her anger subsided as she saw the state of him, hair matted with blood, his clothes torn and filthy. She noticed the piece of metal in his hand as she gently pulled him to his feet.

She didn't notice the figure a few feet away, watching them vanish into thin air. Nor did she notice the rose, the redness darkening into scarlet as it dried in the autumnal sunshine.

15: Barr-Byzhan

Dagre-Frigh, Sennith 2 / 7, Suncycle Teshr

The first cases emerge in the Broken Hemisphere, so have little impact on us. The RAD447/Z disorder— or 'the Madness' as it will come to be known— affects only the Broken, the Uncivilised and Native Byzhans, none of whom have wealth or electoral privileges. The Establishment—and by extension the Citizens of Barr-Byzhan—only start to take notice when the first cases of the Madness occur in the citadels. Vidcasts of the dead and dying soon emerge; horrific images of Byzhans that are skeletal shadows of their former selves, bawling like the Youngest one moment and roaring with untamed aggression the next. The initial symptoms are small and apparently harmless—loss of appetite; an unsightly but painless rash on the neck or limbs; a slight memory loss; moments of untampered emotion. Then the disease takes hold; emotional barriers collapse, perception of the world blurs, crumbles into chaos. Victims of the Madness find themselves unable to digest food, their bodies attack themselves from within, organs collapse. Finally, they become little more than animals. Death is inevitable and painful.

It doesn't take long for Establishmentor Hatch to publicly link the Madness to the Not Like. The emotional outbursts and loss of control among the dying make the connection all too obvious. Isn't this what they always warned us against? The Not Like corrupting our Youngers with their immoral behaviour was bad enough; now an horrific disease signalling the complete collapse of Barr-Byzhan society they've always craved?

The high numbers of cases amongst the Not Like adds fuel to Establishmentor Hatch's allegations. The Commemorative Gardens become heavy with the violet headstones that denote Not Like corpses... until the Establishmentor is advised to close the Gardens to victims of the Madness after rumours of post-mortal contamination—an impossibility of course. But an invaluable weapon in their armoury for the War they're waging on us.

Hatch-G-Mah wins battle after battle with the minimum of effort or resistance. Not long after the Commemorative Gardens are closed to the dead Not Like, the Medical Facilities refuse admission to the dying. The already segregated wards are destroyed and the patients transferred to especially constructed palliative units in the Broken Hemisphere. The Establishmentor assures us that they are doing 'everything possible' to support the experts' sterling work in researching and defeating the Madness, whilst protecting the normal, Creator-fearing Citizens from infection.

With the majority of the infected in or on their way to the palliative units, Hatch-G-Mah passes a law that makes it a criminal act to promote being Not Like as a lifestyle choice.

Their war is won.

On the cycle that the law is passed, I hear your voice for a second time. This time I don't dismiss it as a dream. This time I'm wide awake when I hear you, and there are consequences.

It's the cycle of Barram-N-Coll's pairbonding service. As they suggested, I've feigned illness to Barram-L, who has gone alone. Knowing that my Primary would not believe or accept my excuse, I've let them believe that I am back in the Temple of the West Pyramid… which is how I come to be wandering along the outer walkway of the citadel dressed once again in my Primary's white robe, the dark scarlet pairbonding sash looking like a bloody wound across my chest. The sun is high in the sky, the heat unrelenting, dust rising from my footwear with every step. Beyond the citadel the desert is vast, lifeless. Occasionally a transport vehicle slices through the whiteness, stirring up clouds of sand in its wake then vanishing over the horizon on its journey to another citadel, or perhaps to the intercontinental transportation hub at the bottom of the mainland.

I am alone.

Then I am not.

Hoo… Jeyms… Plee… spirr… Plee…

They're not words; none that I recognise in any case. What I *do* recognise is the fear, the loneliness. The feeling of being different, of being Not Like. And there it is again: the whispering, the rush of air, the fizz of blue energy filling me, but this time it's even more intense. The air is icier, the taste more intense. Your voice is filling me, overwhelming me… and there's music: a discordant chime, like distant bells, growing closer…

I lose consciousness. I think.

I must have done. Because I have no memory at all of what happened between hearing your voice and waking up at Hoss-Well Point.

16: Earth

'I only saw it for a couple of seconds, but it was definitely alien,' Robert said, dunking a digestive into his tea, then quickly stuffing it into his mouth before it disintegrated.

'Are you *sure*, Robert? You'd just fractured a rib and were losing a lot of blood. It's possible that you were hallucinating.'

'I *wasn't* hallucinating, Carol!' Robert snapped, immediately regretting it. 'Sorry. I'm sorry. I know that I might have imagined stuff in the graveyard, but that creature was real, I promise you.'

Carol pursed her lips slightly.

'What were you *imagining* in the graveyard?' she asked. She had an irritating habit of honing in on emotional stuff, just like his therapist had back in Barcombe Hill. Robert suspected she'd been trained in some sort of psychoanalysis on the Trig.

'Nothing much,' he lied, 'just crazy stuff.'

'Robert, you're definitely not crazy,' Carol said, then added, 'It must be so difficult, being reminded of James.'

'None of this has got anything to do with James!' Robert protested.

'You were at his grave, Robert,' Carol reminded him gently.

'Yes, I know, but...'

Carol reached over and held his hand. He gave in to the gesture; she was only trying to be kind. He longed for Paul, who would have cracked an inappropriate joke, or even John, who would have ignored the emotional aspect of this completely and got on with the job regardless. Carol sensed his reticence and, still holding his hand, suggested: 'Why don't you describe what you saw to TIM and he can run it through his database, try to get a match?'

A quarter of an hour later, because of the compromised state of his database, TIM had only narrowed the identity of the creature down to one of over ten thousand species.

'I could go back,' Robert suggested, 'try to catch it, so that we know what we're up against!'

'Definitely not!' Carol said sternly. 'You're not going anywhere until that wound is healed. And we're not getting involved, remember? We're lying low. Especially considering that TIM is due for a reboot any day now.'

'I wouldn't *exactly* describe it as a 'reboot',' TIM bristled. 'More of a circuit recalibration necessitated by the Trig's new data-system. But it's a necessary step if I'm going to finally overcome the effects of the Tnawi virus. And Carol's right. You would be in considerably more danger if you left the lab whilst I was temporarily off-line.'

'But that thing is killing people!' Robert protested.

'I'm so sorry that it killed your friend,' Carol replied, 'but he was trespassing. That doesn't mean he deserved to die, of course it doesn't, but the village has been evacuated. Maybe the powers-that-be know about the alien, which is why they did it in the first place.'

'There was a sign about the Government declaring it geologically unsafe,' Robert said. 'The church had gone. And I fell into some sort of tunnel, which was where the alien was.'

'There are no records of geological disturbances or subterranean tunnels in the area,' TIM announced, 'Nor are there any official Governmental accounts relating to the evacuation of Barcombe Hill.'

'So *something* dodgy's going on there,' Robert said, 'even if the government didn't know about the alien. What did they tell people when the village was evacuated? It must have been something pretty drastic to make them all leave—especially the old fogeys who've been living there all their lives. They wouldn't have left just because they'd been told the land was unsafe! Johnny's still there. If I can talk to him…'

'No, Robert,' said Carol, 'we'll file a report and send it to the Trig, but that's all.'

'But Carol…'

'Do you want me to get TIM to put a forcefield around you? Because I will, if that's what it takes to keep you safe!'

Robert looked astonished.

'I'm sorry, but I have to protect you. I gave John and Elena my word.'

'I'm sorry too, Carol.'

He snatched his hand away and stood up, painfully.

'Where are you going?'

'To bed, of course. Like a good little boy.'

17: Barr-Byzhan

Dagre-Frigh, Sennith 2/7, Suncycle Teshr

Hoss-Well Point is a desolate outcrop of rock at the lowest tip of the Mainland, which got its name from its resemblance to the Hoss-Well fish, an ugly breed found mostly in the Broken Ocean. Back at planetform, it was a huge ice mountain that burst out from the sea and hardened into sedoposs rock. The first Byzhans worshipped it; a Monastery still stands in the rock's shadow. Its small clerical order, the 'Friars of Hoss-Well', occasionally appear at ceremonial events, holding staffs topped with the fish's image. As a Youngest I was fascinated by its vicious teeth, bared in a grimace that gave the Hoss-Well an impression of forward motion, as if the cleric were holding it back with a lead formed by the rest of their staff. So, when I saw Hoss-Well Point for the first time, I was terrified. It rose ominously above the transportation hub, black against a cloudless white sky, mouth agape as if about to swoop downwards to consume us all.

This cycle the sky is also cloudless but a deep green, and the air is warm. I feel cool sand below me. I sit up and immediately realise that I've been lying on a beach—an illegal act. A tall, thick bulderbramble bush, pleasingly square, trimmed of its flowers, lines the beach, separating it from the Monastery. How long have I been here? More importantly, who brought me here, and how? I'm still wearing my Primary's ceremonial robe, the scarlet sash held in place by a heavy gold pin, which surely would have been stolen if I'd been abducted by Outer Band thieves. Though my head hurts, I can feel no wound, no sign of being knocked out. Standing, unsteadily, I see that the ground is undisturbed except for a vaguely body-shaped area where I was lying. Can I have been here for so long that a fresh bed of sand has formed around me? There are no footprints or vehicle tracks. Was I perhaps thrown from a sea transport vehicle, or dropped from a hover-bus? If it were the latter, wouldn't the sand have been disturbed by its motors? Unless I'd been dropped from a considerable height... in which case I would surely have sustained some sort of injury. But there is none.

And shouldn't the sun be lower in the sky by now? Surely it should be getting dark, even if I was brought here in the fastest transport vessel. I must have been here—or *somewhere* and *then* here—over dark-cyc. And I remember nothing of it. I have no way of telling how long I've been unconscious. And now I'm not only perplexed, I'm scared.

Very scared indeed.

I think about my Designators. Though it's quite possible that my Primary hasn't even noticed my absence, my Secondary will probably be wondering where I am. Unless they've assumed that I stayed over dark-cyc with the Barrams, improbable as that might be. I start to walk along the beach, hoping to find an entrance to the Monastery, where there must at least be a comm-link.

Suddenly it occurs to me that it must have been *you* that knocked me unconscious and brought me here. Were you also responsible for the storm at Barram-N-Coll's Second Naming Ceremony? If you were, why did you do it? And *who are you?* What have I done to deserve this? I will you to speak again, to show yourself, but you do neither. You're toying with me. What have you made me do in the time it must have taken for us to get here, before wiping my memory of the journey?

The further I walk, the more resolved I am to tell my Designators exactly what has happened: that you, whoever you are, have been entirely responsible for my lower grades, that now you've got some strange vendetta against me and that I need help.

I realise with horror that I've been walking through the bulderbramble bush. I've been so distracted by my thoughts that I didn't notice the branches move aside to create a shaded pathway for me. I try to convince myself that you are responsible for this, but I can taste the light at the back of my throat, can feel my fingers tingling with energy. I made it happen.

I sink to my knees and start to weep. If I were to be seen, I would be arrested for showing emotion in a public place, but I don't care. I am a freak of nature. I deserve to be locked up.

'Welcome.'

The voice is deep and benevolent. As I scramble to my feet, the weathered hand that is offered in assistance is smooth and warm. It belongs to a wise Byzhan with a kind face. I guess that they're a cleric, perhaps even a Friar. I feel immediately at ease in their presence, and offer no resistance to their invitation back to the Sacred Monastery of Hoss-Well. As we approach the monastery, the cleric says very little. When they do speak, it's only to comment on the warmth of the air, or the pleasing scent of the gripp flower fields being harvested down on the farm at the water's edge.

The corridors of the Monastery are clean, unicolour, uncomplicated. Every Byzhan that passes us is dressed in the regulatory grey uniform of a lower cleric. They nod in respect to my new guardian, who must indeed be a Friar. They lead me into a large chamber, where we are greeted by a handsome cleric who presents me with a uniform to replace my celebration robes.

'Thank you, Witness Kahl,' the Friar purrs, 'that will be all.'

The handsome cleric bows their head slightly and leaves the room, closing the ancient wooden door gently behind them.

'Do sit down,' says the Friar, indicating a chair.

We sit, and they introduce themself as Friar Coen. Oddly, the lack of regalia and ceremonial gown does little to declericise them. If anything, their simple attire lends weight to their status. Their eyes have the same intense blueness of Coell-J's, so I find it difficult to meet their gaze, even when they tell me that they remember me from the Temple of the West Pyramid. They were one of the higher clerics that took part in Barram-N-Coll's Second Naming Ceremony.

'It was quite a display, wasn't it?' they say. 'I don't think many of the congregation had seen anything like it.'

It takes a moment for their words to sink in.

'You mean that you *had*, Friar?' I ask nervously.

'I've seen many things,' they reply ambiguously. 'The Works of The Creator know no bounds. Since I was called to spread Their Word, I have visited a host of different places and met every type of Byzhan you can imagine…' They pause. I look up and they add, 'I observe all without judgement.'

This is presumably meant to set me at my ease but does the opposite.

'Every Byzhan has the capacity to change, you see,' they continue, 'even Thorrus-J-Remm.'

The mention of Establishmentor Hatch's disgraced rival startles me.

'One might think that someone like Remm would be unreachable,' they say. 'Depraved, lost even, but I found some common ground.'

'You met Thorrus-J-Remm?' I ask.

'And continue to do so,' the Friar smiles. 'Their Holiness considered me the right cleric for the job, and I relished the challenge.'

For a moment we don't speak. A timepiece, something from the Inhibition Era by the look of it, marks the passing seconds with calm indifference.

'The Outer Island Radicals weren't responsible for what happened in the Temple of the West Pyramid,' I blurt out suddenly.

I'm going to tell the Friar everything. Tell them that Barram-N-Coll and I were somehow responsible, that I'm Not Like, that I have sinned.

'I know they weren't,' they reply simply.

I am speechless.

'You… know?' I repeat eventually. 'But if you know, why didn't you tell the Establishmentor? Why was Thorrus-J-Remm arrested?'

Friar Coen smiles.

71

'The Creator works in mysterious ways,' they say enigmatically. 'If Remm hadn't entered into Readjustment Therapy, I wouldn't have had the opportunity to participate in that process, and most probably wouldn't be here to help you this cycle, uh…'

'Daghu-N.'

They lean forward on their heavy chair, the wood creaking gently as they say:

'You see, Daghu-N, The Creator made you like every other Byzhan, to be a normal Citizen and do everything that is expected of you. But somewhere along the way you were broken, Daghu-N, and that's what we're going to explore. We're going to find out how you got broken and hold it up to The Creator.'

It's true. I do feel broken. Unnatural. But how can the Friar tell? Is their connection to The Creator so strong that they can see inside my mind, just as I could see inside Coel-J's? Surely that would imply that the Friar is Not Like as well?

I dismiss the idea. They have a Calling. The two states of being are completely incompatible.

'I'd like you to think of your life like an ice mountain, Daghu-N. The tiny part above water is your unnatural affinity with the Wild side of yourself and of our world. The larger part below the surface is everything that's hindering your natural growth into a fully developed Citizen. What we've got to do is melt the ice mountain…'

And so it begins.

18: Earth

Thursday 22nd October, 2009

Carol always was a 'good little girl'. Always did what she was told, always finished her homework on time, always helped her mother with the washing up and adhered to her father's rule that 'children should be seen and not heard.' She spent much of her childhood alone, hiding from the rows in her tiny, pink bedroom, where she could lose herself in drawings and fantasy, or wandering through the lush meadows behind their estate, watching her imaginary friends wading through muddy streams and up dirty branches to reunite blackbirds' eggs with the nests they'd fallen from. She'd never have dared to inflame her parents' wrath by climbing the trees herself of course; that was George, Dick and Julian's job. Carol, Anne and Timmy the dog would settle themselves at a distance, making daisy chains and dividing out imaginary cake wrapped in imaginary greaseproof paper that imaginary Nanny had popped into her faithful old biscuit tin.

Only once had Carol taken the lead in her woodland adventures. By then, Julian and the gang had metamorphosed into John, Susan, Titty, Roger and Bridget. They'd been uncharacteristically disinclined to help Carol when she'd discovered an injured baby badger underneath one of her favourite beech trees, so she'd been forced to take action herself. Certain that the poor little thing would evoke the same compassion in her mother as it had done in Carol, she'd wrapped it up in her cardigan and carried it home. The tempestuous reaction and punishments that ensued ensured that Carol never took the lead again… until her imaginary friends finally became real. Julian made his final transition into John, Timmy into TIM and Carol left home. She wasn't alone anymore.

Her parents showed not a glimmer of understanding of, or support for, her decision; by then she was old enough to take on the role of surrogate housewife to both of them, seeing that her mother's illness had rendered her physically incapable. Later, though she was invited to the funeral, she wasn't encouraged to attend.

Carol had found herself back then. Her *real* self. The Carol without compromise, who only obeyed the rules that she agreed with, who was seen *and* heard.

Yes, Carol was always a good little girl… until she wasn't.

'What is it?' Robert asked, puffy-eyed and miserable. 'I can't have done anything wrong; I've been asleep!'

'I know, Robert,' she replied. 'Despite having every reason to break the rules, you haven't. You've been as good as gold, we both have. I think it's time we weren't.'

19: Barr-Byzhan

Dagre-Math, Sennith 0/6, Suncycle Pendh

I sleep in a small cell with one small window and a bare, stone floor. On the cycle I arrived, I hid my Primary's gold pin and scarlet sash beneath a loose brick beneath the window. I'm not sure why. Nor am I sure how long ago that was. Time has lost its meaning here. Its passing in the monastery is marked by the mournful toll of the Great Bell in the tower, the simple meals eaten in silence at sundown and by sleep. The slightly bitter liquid that we are given to accompany the food is, Witness Kahl assures me, a mild but effective sedative that will help us dull any unsavoury emotion that our abhorrent nature might thrive on. It does its job well. Since I entered the Monastery, I've had no desire to repeat the experiences I had with Coell-J. The unnatural connection with plantlife that I felt in the untampered Wildland is negligible. If any of the other 'Seekers of Truth' are Not Like, they don't show it.

We are all treated equally, although each Friar is assigned a Witness who assists them in their duties. It's an honour which, though unacknowledged, gives them a higher status, as well as chambers that must be somewhere else in the Monastery, away from our basic cells.

When we are not eating or sleeping, we are summoned to the Hall of Contemplation, where Friar Coen tutors us in the Word of The Creator and will occasionally choose one of us for Confessional. I've heard that the gruelling process, though not always wholly effective, is at the very least illuminating. Witness Kahl tells me that some confessors, after revealing shocking details about their younghood experiences, are considered 'beyond redemption' and transferred to an asylum for Total Reprogramming.

'Name the moment, Seeker Daghu!' Friar Coen commands, when it is finally my turn.

Their voice loses its calming tone, their face its kindness. Instead they are sharp and focussed. The other Seekers filed out of the Hall when my name was called, secretly grateful not to have been chosen, intrigued by the Truths that will inevitably be revealed.

Only the Friar, their Witness and I remain. Though I convince myself that I have nothing to hide—that I was the victim, not the instigator, of Coell-J's debauched activity in the wildland—part of me fears some dark hidden secret coming to light, something that even I am unaware of.

'Name the moment!' Friar Coen repeats, then the questioning takes an unexpected turn. 'Name the moment when you were unnaturally abused!'

I'm shocked. I look questioningly at Witness Kahl, whose face remains impassive.

'Abused?' I repeat, unable to see the experiences with Coell-J as abusive, though I realise that they were immoral.

'Name the moment that your Primary Designator first led you along the Path of Darkness,' Friar Coen insists.

'My... Primary?' I stutter. 'They never... I don't understand what you mean, Friar. My Primary doesn't know anything about... They never *abused* me. There was never a *moment,* never!'

The moment of violence on the day I learnt the Obligations? Was that abuse?

'Never?'

'No!' I cry.

'None that you can *remember,*' the Friar insists, 'because your Secondary protected you from it.'

I don't understand.

'Your Secondary protected you from *your Primary!*' they continue. 'It's true, Seeker Daghu! You know it is! And so does The Creator!'

'I wasn't *abused!*'

'The Creator can see it all, Seeker Daghu, They love you, and They *will* forgive you!'

Despite the dulling effect of the pacification drugs, I feel my anger rising.

'Forgive me?? I haven't done anything wrong!'

Shameful moments gather to accuse me, flavoured by the nagging memories of the times I've longed to relive them: Coell-J and I coercing the Wildland into cavorting in the intoxicating blue light of object manipulation; the bulderbramble bush parting for me down on the beach; seeing into

78

Barram-N-Coll's mind at the Ceremony... I *have* done wrong. The Creator sees it all. How can The Creator forgive me for all those sins? Will They forgive Coell-J as well? Or are we both beyond redemption?

'Your Secondary was overprotective of you, am I right?' Friar Coen is on a roll now, pacing up and down the aisle in front of me. Why are they so focussed on my Designators when I am the sinner? My Secondary would never have sinned, never have done anything to hurt me, they only ever wanted what was best for me. And I would have shamed them, if they ever knew.

'They swamped you with unnatural affection, they protected you from your Primary...'

'They didn't *need* to protect me from my Primary!' I cry. 'My Primary was *never there*!!'

Friar Coen stops in his tracks as my tears begin to flow. Open emotions: another abnormality, another sin.

'They...' I sob, 'they were never there...'

The Friar nods to Witness Kahl, walks slowly over towards me and rests their hand on my shoulder.

Well done, Seeker Daghu, they whisper, although I swear they're not moving their lips.

20: Earth

'The sign is made from FB-Z,' TIM announced as soon as the scan had finished, 'A metal found only in the Western Sector. I'm afraid that, because my database was compromised by the Tnawi virus, I can't be any more precise than that.'

'Western Sector?' Robert repeated. Geography wasn't his strongest point. 'You mean, uh, America?'

Carol smiled.

'He actually means the Western sector of the known Universe,' she explained. 'It's geographically meaningless, but Timus insisted that the original Universal Cartographers label the various sections with names that the common Federation citizen would understand. It was one of his little quirks. TIM knows full well that we don't use them anymore, but... Well, Timus and TIM share a lot of quirks.'

'What is important,' TIM added, 'is that the sign didn't originate on Earth.'

'So, aliens put up the fence?' Robert concluded, wide-eyed. 'Aliens evacuated Barcombe Hill?'

'It's possible.' Carol shrugged. 'I'm afraid it's also possible that the village wasn't evacuated at all.'

'You mean they killed everyone?'

'It would explain why there are no Governmental records of the evacuation,' TIM confirmed.

Robert felt sick.

'But why? I don't understand,' he said, thinking of everyone he knew that might have been murdered. Theresa, her therapist. Theresa's girlfriend. Mrs Lidster from the Post Office. That weird kid who always seemed to be on the swings with her mobile phone every time he and Andy came back from the cinema in the next village. She would have been the first to go; caught unawares and defenceless in the playground, dragged underground and eaten, just like Stevie.

'But the one I saw,' Robert continued, shuddering again at the memory of it. 'It was an *animal*. It could hardly have put signs or fences up. It doesn't make any sense...'

'The creature you saw might have been another species,' Carol conjectured, 'A pet, maybe, or...'

'A guard dog!'

Carol nodded grimly.

'You may be right,' said TIM. 'Look at the way the sign has been bent out of shape, and the indentations in the metal.'

Robert gasped.

'Teeth marks!'

21: Barr-Byzhan

A mooncycle after my Confessional, Friar Coen invites me into their work chamber.

'You were never 'Not Like', Seeker Daghu,' they say. 'You simply never had a Primary Designator. That's what broke you.'

What they're saying seems implausible, yet truthful at the same time.

'I know you hate them now; I know you blame them, but that's all right,' they assure me, hand on my shoulder again.

'We're not allowed to hate,' I say. 'It's a sin.'

'The Creator permits us to hate Kemmonos, the King of Demons, and the sinful thoughts that they infect us with.'

I hate Kemmonos, that is true. Everyone does.

'You have a desire for a Primary figure in your life and it's been perverted, because that's what happens. Without the proper guidance from a Primary Designator, you've found yourself turning towards the uncontrolled, you've given in to those untampered emotions thinking they're the answer you've been seeking, but I promise you, they're not.'

It's true, I have been searching for answers, without even knowing what the questions are.

'Our world can be a dark place and someone like you can be drawn to the darkest parts of it, *because you're broken.* The Creator can put you back together again. They can help you find that missing Designator.'

'My Primary, you mean?' I ask, shakily.

'No, they're gone now.' Friar Coen shakes their head. 'They abandoned you and you hate them for it, of course you do. It's that hatred that's made you the way you are. But we can find someone better for you than your Primary. The Creator can give you a healthy Primary relationship so that you can heal. And when that happens, your immoral feelings will go away.'

They smile and lay their hand on my shoulder again and look me straight in the eye and at that moment I trust them more than I've ever trusted anyone. They are going to lead me out of the immoral way of life that I've strayed into against my will.

'In a way you'll be reborn,' they say. 'You'll adapt, you'll grow. The Creator knows everything you're going through and They will change you, Seeker Daghu.'

Thursday 22nd October, 2009

'Let's be clear about this,' Carol said, clipping a stun gun to her belt. 'We jaunt in, we find Johnny and… uh…'

'Andy,' said Robert, pulling on the backpack that contained two matter transport belts and a medikit, should they need it. 'If he's there.'

'Andy, yes, of course. We find them, we jaunt them out, and that's it, for the moment. No heroics, no creature-hunting; we're on a rescue mission. Once we're sure that everybody's out of danger, we can alert the Trig and let them take over from there. Robert? Robert, are you listening?'

His face had turned white, his backpack was hanging from his shoulder, his mouth drooped slightly open… but it was his eyes that shocked Carol most of all. His pupils had narrowed to the tiniest of dots; the rest of his eyes were gleaming white.

'Robert?' Carol asked again, to no response, 'TIM, what's happening to him? What's going on?'

'I'm not sure, Carol,' TIM replied.

Robert appeared to shimmer with blue energy, as if he were a television image coming in and out of focus.

23: Barr-Byzhan

For the first time, my life seems simple. Living in the Sacred Monastery of Hoss-Well, under the daily guidance of the Friar, I've left all the complications of my past life behind me. This pursuit of The Creator's Wisdom and Truth is my new path, the one I was meant to follow. Friar Coen and my fellow Truth-Seekers are my new Designation unit.

I learn a lot about the Sacred Texts, and about hating the Byzhan who caused my temporary aberration—My False Primary—by not being there. Friar Coen was right—it's good to despise someone other than myself, which is, I understand, what I've been doing up to now. Because what I've been hating wasn't actually *me;* what I've been hating was what Kemmonos put *into* me, with my False Primary Designator's help. By abandoning me, they let the King of the Dark World in.

Kemmonos created the Not Like as a disease to bring about the downfall of The Creator's magnificent kingdom.

In a moment of candour, Friar Coen confesses that they too were diseased, before they saw the Light of The Creator's Wisdom. We're walking through the Monastery cloisters as the sun is setting. The air is warm, the sweet scent of gripp flowers wafting across from the farm and insects buzzing in and out of the carefully manicured fever fruit trees that provide our nourishment on feast cycles.

'You were... Not Like?' I whisper.

I feel foolish and wonder if my curiosity merits a punishment. I've only been in the solitude cell once but am loathe to repeat the experience.

'I apologise, Friar,' I say, lowering my head in penitence.

'There's no need, Seeker Daghu,' they reply calmly. 'Yes, I was Not Like once. I led a misguided life full of transitory pleasures and misbelief.'

Friar Coen lays their hand on my cheek. I blush without knowing why. They frown suddenly, wish me a cursory good dark-cyc and walk off into the shadows. A moment later, a door slams. I am left alone in the cloisters.

24: Earth

Thursday 22ⁿᵈ October, 2009

James?

They were back in the desert, the air still and stiflingly hot.

86

James, look at me!

James's back was burning, the skin bubbling into blisters, his hair curling, steaming in the heat.

It's me. It's Robert. Please, look at me!

The sand was shifting under their bare feet, snaking around their toes, dancing up their calves.

I've missed you.

And now it leapt over them, a mighty wave of dust that smashed into the dunes in front of them.

James...

Robert knew what came next.

Turn round, James! Turn round!

The dunes collapsed in upon themselves, a vast hole roaring open in front of them.

Please, James!

Energy screamed from deep inside the planet, ancient power hungry for sacrifice.

I can't lose you again! Let it take me!!

And as James stepped into the fireball, he turned; this time he turned, smiled and spoke to him:

I lived, Robert. I survived.

Robert's eyes snapped open.

'Robert!'

The energy vanished and he collapsed, the backpack clattering onto the floor beside him. Carol rushed to his side, knelt down and cupped his face with her hands. He was still pale, but his eyes were back to normal. His cheeks were damp with tears.

'J… James!' he stuttered, 'I saw James! It was him, Carol! He's still alive!'

25: Barr-Byzhan

Dagre-Laugh, Sennith 2/7, Suncycle Pendh

Looking back, it's easy to see how Friar Coen manipulates the situation, how they use their clerical power to make me believe that they can provide the healthy Primary relationship I've been lacking. I'm hungry for their approval (and, by extension, The Creator's blessing) and—though I try to deny it— for the Not Like experience I had with Coel-J in the Wildland. As the Friar manoeuvres me from a common Seeker to replace Kahl as their Witness, it makes sense to move me out of my frugal cell and into the Friar's opulent chamber, with its comfortingly soft floor covering and awe-inspiring views. We watch the sun set magnificently behind Hoss-Well Point and talk openly about the lives we've left behind. I delight in colourful tales of their experiences before they were called to the Clericdom.

It's an act of unanticipated intimacy. Only once do I see Seeker Kahl, walking in line to their duties in the gripp fields, look up towards our window and flash me a look of... what? Jealousy? Disdain? I mention it to Friar Coen and Kahl spends a sennith in the solitary cell as punishment.

It's not long before the Friar is excusing me from the pacification drug and offering me a gripp-flower infusion in its place. Under its influence, one intimate act leads to another and, in the privacy of our chamber, they project their memories into my head, we manipulate flowers with our minds, and more. Lulled into a more or less permanent sense of calm and security, I accept every gift, every delicious meal and every proposition without resistance. This, the Friar assures me, is The Creator's will. Together we are controlling and containing the evil that Kemmonos put into us by allowing it into our chamber and no further. I vow to maintain the vital secrecy, knowing that there will be a place for me at The Creator's side when our mortal lives are at an end.

I witness Confessionals, just as Kahl did. I see Friar Coen break down each new seeker's defences to reveal the truth they wish to find within them. Like Kahl, I remain impassive, playing my part well, only revealing my thoughts and feelings to the Friar as we mock them later, dizzy on infusion.

And then eventually Friar Coen bores of me. Rather, they bore of my reliance on the infusion, they bore of my Younghood memories that bubble to the surface when they're projecting theirs into my head, they bore of the passing fantasies I indulge in about the occasional new Seeker, despite having those same fantasies themself. One in particular, a fresh-faced Dravvhan called Waldh-H, starts to obsess them—I see it clearly in the Hall of Contemplation. Then, when Seeker Waldh is chosen for Confessional, I, as Witness, know exactly what is about to happen next. The Friar lays their hand on the confessor's shoulder and I hear them whisper *Well Done, Waldh-H*. Later, head buzzing with infusion, I challenge them about it and am rewarded by a sennith in the solitary cell.

In my cell, I dream that I hear your voice again:

Aye-kahn! Louss-U! Gayne! Lettitay! Kmee!!

Is it a dream or is it a vision? I've no way of telling. On waking, I remember every word, although I understand none of them.

When I emerge from solitary, Waldh-H has taken my position, and I am escorted silently back to my old cell. The key turns in the lock: one solitary cell exchanged for another. Loosening the brick by the window, I retrieve my Primary's scarlet sash and gold pin. They're covered in dust. I roll the pin between my fingers thoughtfully. Were they really the demon that Friar Coen made them out to be? The last few senniths have made me doubt everything the Friar taught me. I unravel the sash and wrap it round me, securing it with the pin.

It's an act of defiance for which I'll probably be punished.

A plateful of bland food and a flask of pacification drug sits on the small table at my bedside. I ignore the food, pick up the flask and empty it, watching the liquid splash onto the floor. It creates a pleasingly unnatural pattern in the stone's contours. It occurs to me that Barr-Byzhan is *full* of the unnatural and disordered. If The Creator made our world, why did They allow it to contain such wild perversion?

If They ever existed, that is.

I lie on the rough sleeping bench, missing the silken sheets of the Friar's chamber. I watch the last of the liquid dribble away towards the locked door and wonder what they have planned for me. If I'm to go the way of Witness Kahl, I can expect more spells in solitary and menial work that reflects my new lower status.

I close my eyes and drift into an uneasy sleep,

26: Earth

'And there was evidence of temporal disturbance,' TIM concluded. 'Only faint, but substantial enough to register on my secondary scan.'

'Could it have been one of the Guardians?' Carol inquired.

'Malachi?' asked Robert, remembering his disturbing trip to an alternative future. 'Could it be that James is reaching out to me from a Universe where he didn't sacrifice himself? Is that possible?'

'It is possible,' TIM conceded, 'but improbable. And in this case, highly unlikely.'

'Why?' asked Robert, haughtily.

'Because accompanying the temporal disturbance was a trace signature that I did recognise. That of the late President Dracquell's Universal Transportation Network.'

Carol gasped.

'But that was destroyed!' she argued.

'*Paul* destroyed it,' Robert added sullenly, remembering the ensuing emotional turmoil.

'It's possible that not all of it was destroyed,' TIM said calmly. 'Perhaps a few corridors remained partially intact but disconnected after the explosion.'

'And that's how James is talking to me?' Robert surmised, 'So all we need to do is find this end of the corridor and travel along it!'

'I'm afraid it's not that simple,' TIM warned.

'And we have other things to do first,' Carol reminded him. 'If you feel up to it?'

'Of course I do!' Robert replied, sure of one thing. James was alive, somewhere in time and space, and they would be reunited as soon as humanely possible. If it meant enlisting someone else's help—Malachi's maybe—then so be it.

Robert felt utterly *alive* again.

He hopped onto the jaunting pad, unable to hide his new enthusiasm. Carol smiled gently, deciding to avoid dampening his spirits by focussing on practicalities.

'From what Robert's told us, we should be safe if you jaunt us into the, uh, Devil's Nook,' she instructed TIM, then looked across at Robert, 'Ready?'

27: Barr-Byzhan

Dagre-Laugh, Sennith 2/7, Suncycle Pendh

I open my eyes.

I'm not in my cell anymore.

There's a terrifying noise: a high-pitched scream that assaults my ears with its unnatural complexity and seems to have no beginning or end. Struggling to ignore it, I feel the cool, gentle touch of sand below me. Am I back on the beach? I roll my head to the side and see that it's not sand, but finely broken down sedoposs, the dark blue rock that, processed and polished, becomes blackstone. My head is pounding, my mouth dry. How long have I been here?

Did you bring me here?

I sit up. I'm on a clumsily constructed walkway. The high-pitched screaming seems to come from bulderbramble bushes and feverfruit trees which have grown into an unnaturally tangled mass of vegetation, like they did in the Wildland. I stand. As I stumble forward along the walkway, a bird flutters out of the brambles and flies off with a petulant squawk. I realise that the screaming sound is actually birdsong. But it's not just one type of bird singing, it's several, jumbled together in a tangle of calls that are as unnatural, *illegal,* as the mess of vegetation. The sun's warmth caresses my neck. Unlike the clean, dry atmosphere of the Monastery, the air here is alive with a cacophony of smells: the sweetness of damp soil dances with the acidic tang of bulderbramble flowers. Unlike the Wildland's unnerving confusion of scents, though, this place somehow offers serenity, as if the smells were cavorting in a natural order, if there can be such a thing.

Could it be that you've brought me here out of kindness? An act of generosity? That somehow you sensed the confusion I felt back at the Monastery and are offering me some kind of escape?

Hello!

The voice comes from directly behind me. I turn quickly, subconsciously raising my hands in defence. But there's nobody. I *definitely* heard the voice. It wasn't the voice I heard you use before, it was slightly older, with the hint of a Drahvvan accent. Have you disguised yourself?

'Hello?'

My greeting is met with silence and no movement. Even the plantlife at the side of the walkway is still.

Hello, Daghu-N.

Once again, the voice comes from behind me. Your new voice. Once again, I turn to see nobody.

'Who are you?' I demand. '*Where* are you?'

I'm Addh-C, you reply, *there's no need to be frightened.*

'I'm not frightened!' I reply haughtily, feeling foolish to be talking to thin air. I look for wires, hidden speakers, but can see none hidden in the immediate area.

Aren't you? you ask, with a disarming air of sarcasm. *Well, congratulations, Daghu-N! I was terrified when I had my first thoughtshare. I thought I'd caught the Madness or something! Not that the Madness existed back then. Forgive me, I get a little unfocused when I'm welcoming new Sups. I don't know why the Guru always chooses me to do it—it'd far better suit someone less excitable, if you ask me. Maybe that's the idea. Perhaps they're hoping I'll learn to calm down a bit eventually. Hasn't happened yet though! And if you're as special as we think you are… Don't worry, I'll be with you soon, I'm nearly out of the wildwood, then we can mouthspeak…*

'For The Creator's sake!' I cry. 'What in the Dark World are you talking about? And where are you?!'

Here! you laugh back, *just coming out of the wildwood!*

Then I see you, up the hill, waving down at me as you emerge from the trees. Only it isn't you, of course. The waving Byzhan is tall, with an unruly mop of mousey hair, legs seemingly too long for their body. In time I'll fondly tease Addh-C for the way they plod round with all the grace of a Gargantuan shortneck. In time we'll see the real animals together, in the wild; Addh-C will laugh at the way the shortnecks seem to mimic them. By then I'll understand the beauty of Addh-C's awkward gait, but now it irritates me.

'Who are you?' I demand as they reach me. 'And where in the Dark World am I? Did you bring me here?'

'That's a lot of questions,' Addh-C smiles. 'Come on, I'll try to answer them on the way to the Sanctuary.'

I stand my ground. Their clothing is dirty, mismatched, illegal. They look like a perverted.

'I'm not going anywhere with you!' I spit at them.

They nod, smiling.

'Then have a nice dark-cyc. I'd sleep standing up if I were you, if you manage to sleep at all. Those bushes are full of bulderbramble rodents. They're friendly enough during the cycle but at dark-cyc they'll sink their teeth into anything that moves.'

Addh-C turns to walk away. I'm incensed.

'You can't just… Come back, now!!'

They carry on walking up the hill.

Back!!

I say the word, but not out loud. It leaves my mind and then reforms in Addh-C's. Just like the Friar's memories travelled into my head. And Coell-J's before that. Addh-C stops walking.

That's more like it.

They turn as they speak, but their lips aren't moving.

It's not far to the Sanctuary. I can explain everything there.

How this happen? my mind asks theirs. *What this?*

This, my friend, is thoughtsharing. It's this way, Daghu-N.

We walk in silence—but not—up the hill, towards the wildwood.

How you know name? I ask. I seem incapable of forming complete sentences.

You told me, when you arrived on the Island. Us, I mean.

Who us?

There are forty-nine of us at the moment. Fifty when you decide to stay.

I don't respond to that. I don't have the words yet.

My initial reaction to the Sanctuary is odd, in that, though I've never been here before, or seen anything like it, it seems familiar. No, more than familiar, I *know* it. The Courtyard in which we're standing has either been roughly hewn out of rock or is an ancient formation: a bubble of air in a volcanic eruption maybe. The walls are festooned with bulderbramble bushes, untamed, their vibrant pink flowers giving the space a strange warm glow. I know, without having to climb the uneven steps on either side of the courtyard, that above us are a network of chambers, each tailored to the tastes of their inhabitants, none adhering to the strict aesthetic guidelines laid down by the Establishment. I know also that a place in one of those chambers has been reserved for me and I know what it will look like when I have decided to stay here. It's an unsettling feeling.

'Yes,' Addh-C nods, thankfully using their real voice—'mouthspeaking'—again, 'I felt the same when I first arrived. I'd seen every chamber before, every corridor, every tree, every crack in every wall. We all had. But that's impossible, isn't it? Unless of course we dreamshared. That's a thing too.'

I feel suddenly dizzy and reach for Addh-C's support. It's as though somebody's slapped me in the face; no, not in the face, across the side of my head. The sensation passes after a while, but I'm starting to find the noise in the Courtyard overwhelming. It's obvious that the Sanctuary is inhabited by different designation strata, but none of them have adopted the silence required by a gathering of cultures. Far from it. There's conversation, bodily contact punctuated by vocal reaction, even the sound of open laughter. I've never seen or heard anything like it.

A bell chimes.

'Shall we eat?' Addh-C suggests. 'Guru!'

They bellow to a white-haired Citizen who crosses the Courtyard and smiles; the same, apparently kind, smile as Addh-C's, though I'd guess that theirs is less likely to transform into a smirk. It seems contrived somehow. I dislike them immediately. They are accompanied by two Citizens. All three are dressed with no attention to line, symmetry or permissible colour co-ordination.

'This is Clahh-M,' Addh-C smiles proudly, 'the Guru!'

'Welcome to the Sanctuary,' Clahh-M says. 'I hope Addh-C hasn't been unnerving you. They never did learn how to restrain their emotions. Probably because they were so young when they upgraded.'

Addh-C and one of Clahh-M's associates share a look which lasts long enough for me to suspect that they are *thoughtsharing*.

'...which I would have to have unlearned anyway!' Addh-C says to me incongruously, as if I've been party to their conversation.

Clahh-M shoots them a strange look.

'My apologies, Guru,' Addh-C says, 'I forgot.'

Before I have the chance to ask them what they've forgotten, Clahh-M suggests that we should eat. They indicate that I should lead the way. Though it makes no sense, I instinctively know where we're going.

28: Earth

Friday 23rd October, 2009

Carol and Robert materialised in a dark, silent bar in Barcombe Hill. Flicking her torch on, Carol saw that heavy wooden tables had been leant against the windows, their underbellies stained and cracked, covered with grime, dust and lumps of blackened chewing gum, stuck there in innocent days when the locals' greatest fear was that they might come last in the pub quiz, not that they'd die before they'd finished their pints. In one corner of the room there was a motley collection of electronic devices, tins of food, clothing, bits of silverware and other stolen goods, piled haphazardly and without care. Empty cans and bottles littered the floor, along with remnants of the food that had accompanied their contents.

Carol started at a sudden noise, then relaxed as she saw a small rat scuttling across the floor and into the Scavenger Gang's pile. Robert wandered over to a door and was surprised when it opened without protestation. Beyond it was a small corridor leading to a fire exit, possibly the one that he'd seen Johnny Turner emerge from the day before.

Better not, Carol warned him as he reached for the bar that would open it.

He nodded and was about to retrace his steps to the bar when they were both blinded by another torch, being shone at them from the open doorway.

'What the hell…?' someone exclaimed.

'It's all right, we're here to help you,' Carol offered, raising her arms in surrender.

'You're the one I saw with Stevie!' the voice in the dark said, his torchlight landing on Robert's face. 'Where is he?'

'Johnny? Johnny Turner?'

'How the hell do you know my name?'

'It's Robert. Robert Mitchell, from school!'

There was a brief pause, then:

'Well, that's bloody perfect, that is!'

'Johnny…'

'Ssh!'

Johnny flicked his torch out, Carol and Robert

did the same, and they were consumed by darkness. Outside, somewhere, the rumbling of tyres on rubble announced the arrival of what sounded like a large vehicle. It hissed to a halt. Two doors opened, followed by the crunch of heavy boots as several people disembarked. There was unintelligible muttering, then more footsteps, moving closer.

'Back into the Nook!' Johnny hissed.

They fumbled their way into the bar, where the little light seeping through gaps around the home-made barricades revealed that Johnny was unarmed and heading towards the pile. Robert slipped the backpack off and was about to reach into it for the teleportation belts when the fire exit was kicked violently open. Seconds later, six or seven men burst into the room, lights on helmets.

Johnny pulled a revolver out of a grubby microwave.

The soldiers fired without hesitation.

29: Barr-Byzhan

Dagre-Laugh, Sennith 2/7, Suncycle Pendh

The air of the Eating Hall is swollen with fragrance and noise. The unruly roar of conversation, food being shared on a whim, seemingly dangerous disagreements that suddenly evaporate into piercing howls of laughter, *Byzhans moving from table to table,* all combine to give the appearance of wild animals feasting on a cave full of freshly-slaughtered corpses.

'You're obviously Citizens,' I say, wiping my mouth at the end of what was probably the tastiest meal I've ever eaten. 'Why have none of you got a third name?'

Addh-C laughs, loudly. My Primary would have banished me to my quarters for a sennith for such unsightly behaviour. In here, the transgression seems meaningless.

'Because we're *not* Citizens,' they correct me. 'We don't subscribe to that way of life, not here. We're Not Like, Daghu-N, and proud to be.'

The concept of taking pride in one's perversion is utterly alien to me. My suspicion that Addh-C, Clahh-M and their fellow Islanders are terrorists would seem to be confirmed, although as yet they've shown no signs of any desire to topple Barr-Byzhan's Establishment or destroy civilisation as we understand it.

As I suspected, this is one of the Outer Islands, unpopulated until a suncycle ago, when Clahh-M and a handful of Not Likes landed here in a dilapidated sea transport vehicle, hid in caves for a few senniths then, when they were certain they'd not been followed, started to explore the Island and create their new home. They crafted dwellings out of gullies and holes in the rock so that no passing air transport vehicle could spot them. Clahh-M, the oldest Islander, had been a wildland manipulator back on the mainland; under their expert tuition, new growth was nurtured to form further barriers to the outside world. Clahh-M was then elected 'Guru' by their fellow Not Likes, who left the Island to recruit more of their kind.

It would seem that the Islanders have no intention of returning to civilisation.

'Not until the Infos are ready for us.' Addh-C smiles. 'Which might be some time.'

'Hopefully we'll all live to see it,' Clahh-M says more optimistically. 'If the number of upgrades continues to increase at the current rate.'

'The what?' I ask.

'An upgrade,' Addh-C explains, 'is what we call the progression from Info to Sup.'

'I don't understand what you're talking about.'

Clahh-M then calmly clarifies:

'The Byzhan race is on the verge of a massive genetic change, Daghu-N. 'The Final Upgrade'.

Enlightened geneticists realised this some time ago, but their discoveries were buried, their voice silenced.'

'Of course it was!' Addh-C comments, grabbing a piece of bread and ripping it into two. *After* their allocated food portion has been finished! Once again, I picture my Primary's face and can't help smiling.

'Our race is metamorphosing from Byzhan Inferior to Byzhan Superior,' Clahh-M continues, 'or, as the Establishment would have us see it, from Citizen to Not Like.'

'You call the Not Like 'Byzhan Superior'?' I say, incredulously.

'Of course we do! Because we are!' Addh-C beams.

'We have powers that have lain dormant for generations,' Clahh-M says. 'Thoughtsharing, nature manipulation and, very rarely, the power to placeroam.'

'To what?'

'To move yourself from one part of Barr-Byzhan to another,' Addh-C explains excitedly. 'As far as we know, it's only happened once before, until…'

Clahh-M holds up a hand to stop Addh-C midsentence. Their skin is weathered, their palm scarred. The protruding veins suggest that they are even older than they seem. Old enough to be taken to an End of Life Foundation, perhaps, unless they'd chosen to follow the clerical path, where age is tolerated rather than properly hidden out of sight. Could this outlandish theory—that the Not Like are some sort of superior race—be a story concocted by Clahh-M to justify stepping out of normal society and avoiding the Foundation? If it is, then Addh-C believes the lie wholeheartedly, as I discover later that dark-cyc.

I have been assigned to the same crude living pod as them. The chamber is hollowed out of bare rock, lit by six flaming torches that jut out of heavy metal brackets close to the ceiling, out of reach, the light giving the peculiar impression of the pod being open to the sky. The walls are decorated by an unsophisticated painting of a landscape that Addh-C tells me is supposed to be the gripp flower fields of their younghood. When I marvel at their Designators allowing them to go anywhere near untampered nature, they shrug and say that they were the youngest of four siblings. I suspect that this is why they were so far behind in their studies before they came to the Island.

You could be right there, Daghu-N!

I'm shocked by Addh-C's intrusion into my thoughts.

'Did I give you permission to read my mind?!' I snap at them.

They blush.

'Sorry,' they say, 'force of habit. The Guru is always telling me off for doing it. But then I've always found it difficult to follow the rules! Not that there *are* many rules here. Rules are for Infos. When the Sups take control, we won't need them.'

I find their sheepish smile endearing despite my irritation at the intrusion. Their pose is languid, head resting against a large, multi-coloured pillow, their unkempt curls adding an extra layer to the erratic pattern. Everything about Addh-C—their splayed limbs, their changeable expressions, everything—is disordered, chaotic, enchanting.

Suddenly I feel incredibly tired. The warm allure of sleep threatens to overcome me before I've had the opportunity to recount the Obligations. I've got so many questions to ask Addh-C, but they'll have to wait—already my eyelids are heavy. I haul myself to my feet at the exact moment that I taste the whispering blue energy and four of the flames flicker off at Addh-C's bidding.

Me too, they thoughtshare, apologetically adding, 'Sorry! I'm tired too. We can talk in the morning.'

'How am I supposed to recount the Obligations

in the dark?' I ask brusquely.

Addh-C laughs gently, then yawns.

'There's none of that here,' they say, stretching their arms and legs simultaneously. 'Pretty pointless once you realise that The Creator never existed. And all that flapping your arms about is just daft, if you ask me.'

Their smiles pierce me through the half-light. Then, even though they're on the other side of the chamber, and their eyes are already closed, I smell their breath, heavy with spices, feel their lips brush mine and, as the two remaining flames die, hear them whisper a soundless *Sleep well* in the darkness.

I am alone in the dark. It's a darkness I've never experienced before, one in which there is no Creator, there are no rules, no Designators, no inculcators, only Addh-C and me.

I am alone but not alone.

30: Earth

Friday 23rd October, 2009

'They picked me up in that church in Cuckberry; I was just lying there, easy pickings,' Andy said, glaring at Robert. 'So, thanks for that, mate.'

Robert hated being called *mate* but thought it would be churlish to complain, especially as he and Carol had been responsible for Andy's incarceration, albeit indirectly. He rubbed his left shoulder, where the muscles still ached from the Taser darts. Mind you, everything ached now; as effective as TIM's artificial skin grafting had been, the real skin around his head wound was taking time to adjust to the surgery, and his rib was still very tender. He glanced around the room where they'd woken up, ironically one of the old classrooms that he, Andy, Stevie and Johnny had once sat sloshing powder paints onto sweet-smelling paper and whispering naughty limericks to each other whilst Miss Ireland tried vainly to enlighten them about the Battle of Hastings. The room was as filthy and chaotic as the Devil's Nook had been, but at least the windows hadn't been covered, so he could see the odd assortment of inhabitants. There must have been about twenty of them, different ages and sexes, all showing signs of their imprisonment: a woman in her late sixties was nursing an arm that had been put into a sling improvised out of a cardigan; a young boy picked at the dark scab on his left leg that matched a similar wound on his right. Andy himself had an ugly series of bruises that started on his cheekbone and continued down his neck to his collarbone, which jutted out from beneath the blood-stained combat fatigues, making him look almost emaciated. He was a far cry from the plump prankster that Robert remembered from their childhoods. Johnny, too, looked pained and underfed. He was lying on the floor, eyes closed, head resting on a grubby coat that he'd found beneath a pile of broken chairs. Wood splintered, metal legs bent out of shape, they were tiny, broken mementoes of the schoolchildren they'd once held.

'Who are all these people?' Carol asked softly.

'Prisoners of war,' Johnny replied darkly from the floor, without opening his eyes.

'But we're not *at* war,' Robert protested, 'not anymore!'

'Oh no?' Johnny scoffed, 'Tell that to your mate Stevie! Oh, wait a minute, you can't—the idiot went and got himself killed! We all saw *that* coming, didn't we boys?!'

He laughed. Robert looked questioningly at Andy, who shrugged, shaking his head.

'Most of them were arrested at anti-Government rallies,' he said. 'That woman over there's an MP. Liberation party. Bridget Crowley. Used to be a Green, before the invasion.'

Robert looked again at the woman with the broken arm and recognised her. She was deep in conversation with another woman who was dressed in similar fatigues to his friends.

'You mean we're political prisoners?' Carol asked, shocked.

Andy nodded grimly.

'But what's going to happen to us?'

'You don't want to know,' Andy replied.

'Well yes, Andy, we do!' Robert snapped, irritated by his friend's attitude.

Johnny laughed; eyes still closed.

'Still as entitled as ever then!' he sneered. 'Well, you're not so special now, Bobby. You'll end up as dead as the rest of us, sooner or later. I'd put my money on sooner, if I had any.'

'They're going to kill us?' Carol asked.

'Oh no,' Johnny replied, 'That'd be technically illegal, without a trial. Their little pet is going to do it for us.'

'The alien?' asked Robert.

Johnny nodded, opening his eyes.

'Bloodsports.'

31: Barr-Byzhan

In the morning I wake from troubled dreams to find my clerical uniform, my sash and pin gone and a small pile of clothes left in their place. Addh-C urges me to put them on and smiles warmly when I've finished.

'That's more like it,' they say, patting my shirt lightly, then undoing the top button. Their interference should feel like an intrusion, but I find myself welcoming it. Nevertheless, I scowl at them and do the button up again. Their smile widens. A distant whispering seeps into the air, a thin trail of blue light snakes through my hair from behind me and down into my shirt, which unbuttons itself.

'Did you...?' I begin.

Addh-C laughs and leaps out of bed, their unbridled nakedness revealing both Primary *and* Secondary genitalia. Addh-C is even more of a freak than I am. And they've learnt how to manipulate inanimate objects as well, which is baffling.

Nothing is inanimate on a molecular level, they correct me, even though I've made no comment, *and I'm not a 'freak' by the way! Neither are you, Daghu-N.*

113

They bound out of the chamber, their laughter echoing repeatedly down the corridor of rock behind them.

The First Meal is, if anything, even rowdier than last dark-cyc. Once again the food is delicious in a way I've not experienced before, not even in the Friar's chamber.

'If the Sanctuary has no links to the Mainland,' I ponder aloud, 'where does all this food come from? Do you raid passing cargo transport vehicles or something?'

'Of course not!' Addh-C laughs. 'There are growth meadows here, three of them. They give us everything we need.'

After the meal we are left to our own devices. Addh-C and I navigate our way through the narrow gap between the rocks that forms a passageway to the Island's only gripp field. Having smoked gripp throughout their younghood (hardly a surprise) they are keen to pick and process some petals, even though they suspect that the Guru will disapprove. For someone that is apparently preparing their followers for a life without rules (once the Final Upgrade has happened) Clahh-M seems to have established a disproportionate number of them in the Sanctuary. Addh-C is taking me through them as we clamber over rocks, the sun burning a column of light through the gap above us.

No weapons, obviously. No thoughtsharing in the Courtyard, or in any shared spaces in the Sanctuary.

Why that? I ask clumsily, aware for the first time that *thoughtsharing* makes my teeth ache.

It's the Guru's idea. They reason that when the Final Upgrade happens, not all Byzhans will be Sups. They don't want us to lose our ability to mouthspeak, so that the Infos don't feel left out.

Clahh-M's reasoning—or maybe Addh-C's clumsy explanation of it—seems dubious. The sea, distantly smashing against the shoreline, lends a bass-heavy undertone to our silent conversation; a thunderous, doom-like sound.

Object manipulation should only be practised in pairs, and only at the regulated times. That's so we learn to control it. Apparently when they first got together, the Settlers were so excited to be manipulating as a group, they nearly brought the Courtyard roof down!

Settlers?

The original Not Likes that arrived here with the Guru.

One suncycle ago?

That's right. Hey, you're getting better at thoughtsharing already—you managed an adverb!

I yelp as I catch my arm on the thorny branch of a bulderbramble bush poking through the rock wall. The sun illuminates the small cluster of flowers, lending Addh-C's face a yellow hue. They pull a mockingly pitiful expression, as if I'm a Youngest taking their first steps.

'I've never seen bulderbramble bushes growing wild before,' I scowl, rubbing my arm. 'Not under these circumstances in any case.'

'They're not wild,' Addh-C replies. 'The Guru planted them when they first came to the Island. The settlers brought seeds.'

As we scramble further, I become aware of a sweet smell that seems familiar but unplaceable. Addh-C also notices it.

Gripp smoke! they thoughtshare. *Someone's beaten us to it! I bet it's Ritch-U—they were a gripp-head too, back on the Mainland.*

I grimace at the expression, which only reinforces my prejudice about the Outer Banders: a bunch of no-hopers we were warned about at the Facility, all destined for a life of servility in the lower strata. The smell is becoming more intense, its sickly sweetness catching in the back of my throat. It reminds me of my Primary; the unpleasant stink of their robes in the darkness, on that dark-cyc in my younghood.

The forbidden rhyme tickles my memory. I try to focus on perfecting my thoughtsharing, aware that I am doing it to spite... who? Addh-C? My Primary? The *Guru?*

No weapon. No thought. No object, I manage, *No place-roam?*

Addh-C stops, turns, mouthspeaks:

'Like I told you, there's only been one of us who could do that, according to the Guru... until...'

'Until what?'

'Until you.'

I don't understand. Addh-C steps towards me.

'When I heard you arrive,' they say with a new intensity, 'the Guru seem surprised, shocked even. We all saw it in their face, even though they denied it. But it made sense. They usually give us advance notice, you see, and the new Sups usually arrive on a sea transport vehicle, in twos, threes or fours. All illegal landings, of course, but the Guru has a contact at the nearest transportation hub—one of the Settlers I think—they wipe the journeys from the official records. They told us that your arrival *had* been planned, but that it was a last-minute thing, and that Ritch-U and I were to handle your initiation as usual. Before we disabled your emcel, Unn cross-matched it for transits and there was no trace of one! So...'

'What do you mean by *disabling* my—what was it, *emcel?*' I interrupt.

It's Addh-C's turn to be surprised.

'Honestly, Daghu-N, did your Designators told you nothing?! Surely you know that every Youngest is fitted with an MCL as soon as they've learnt the Obligations?'

'MCL? I've never heard of it! What is it?'

'A Microchip Code Locator. How else do you think the Establishment keeps tabs on us all?'

'But... who does it?' I stammer. 'Who fits it?'

'Your Primary of course!'

The inexplicable act of violence in the darkness. I didn't dream it after all. The air is turning cold. I shudder. Addh-C suggests we move onwards.

There's no need to worry, they thoughtshare. *Yours is disabled now. All of our emcels are. Otherwise, they'd know where we are and we'd all be dead within a mooncycle.*

No dead, surely!

Well, rounded up and taken to a Readjustment Institution at least. Hatch-G-Mah and their cronies hate the Sups; they see us as a threat to their power, which I suppose we are, though we're not the kind of threat they think we are. When the Final Upgrade comes, it'll be a bloodless revolution. More of a gentle progression.

You sound like Guru.

Addh-C laughs.

Thank you! Anyway, you didn't come here on any sort of transport, you weren't there one moment and then you were. Place-roaming!

I don't believe them. The air is thick with the stink of gripp smoke now; it's becoming overpowering. Addh-C turns to smile at me. There's a new look in their eyes; I saw it last dark-cyc at the table, directed at Clahh-M. It makes me feel uneasy. Beyond them the passageway is widening—we're nearly at the gripp field, which appears to be shrouded in an early sea mist.

'Is that the gripp field, then?' I ask, nodding towards the hazy sight at the end of the passageway.

Addh-C turns back and walks out into the mist. After a moment I join them. It's not sea-mist. The field has been ravaged by fire, last dark-cyc by the look of it—although there are no flames, the darkened soil is still belching out black smoke. The remnants of a devastated natural crop are little more than black sticks, protruding from the earth at unnatural angles. Dead.

So much for the gripp petals.

'Who's done this?' I mouthspeak.

'I don't know.' Addh-C shrugs. 'A natural phenomenon maybe? Nobody at the Sanctuary would have done it.'

I find this difficult to believe.

'No, Daghu-N,' Addh-C insists, 'they wouldn't. We can't. It's part of our condition. Byzhan Superiors are incapable of harming any living thing. Gripp flowers included.'

I laugh, but Addh-C's expression remains set.

'Clahh-M really has brainwashed you, haven't they?'

For the first time I see a flash of anger cross Addh-C's face. Rather than argue the point, they indicate a large-ish boulder at the edge of the gripp field. The familiar whispering begins, there's a crackle of blue energy and the rock leaps upwards from the burnt soil. It hovers between is, thin fissures of light making it appear fluorescent.

Hit me with it, Addh-C challenges me. I feel a memory flash into my head; one of their younghood memories: a Citizen raising a hand; their Primary, perhaps?

No.

Go on, they urge, *try it!*

With surprisingly little effort, I reach out with my mind and swipe the boulder out of the air. It bounces off the wall and into the dead vegetation with a sharp crack and a resolute thump.

No, I repeat.

We return to the Sanctuary in silence. As soon as we reach the Courtyard, Addh-C is distracted by an audience with the Guru and I am approached by Ritch-U, one of the Sups that greeted me the cycle before. Addh-C's rival gripp-head. They have been assigned to practise object manipulation with me in one of the growth meadows. Although they're not as challenging as Addh-C, I find their company less engaging. I find myself wondering whether Addh-C will be joining us, then try to sublimate the thought, as we were taught to do in the Emotion Sublimation classes at the Facility. In class the aim would be to maintain societal dignity; now I wish to screen my emotions from Ritch-U. They show no sign of having intruded on my thoughts, though. Perhaps the act of intrusion is unique to Addh-C.

And Friar Coen.

I shudder at the memory of them.

Above us, a few greyish moisture clouds break up the deep green sky. Unlike the rest of the Sanctuary, the growth meadow is pleasingly natural and impeccably managed. Straight rows of faultlessly cultivated vegetation form uniform bands of colour, a perfect diamond that would not look out of place in the citadel. At least the Guru has allowed one sign of civilisation here; even they have to admit that not everything the Byzhan Inferiors created is redundant. Everyone has to eat. To the side of each row, smooth pipes glisten in the sunshine. I ask Ritch-U what they are.

'They spread nutrition promoter to the crops,' they explain to me with a sigh, as if I were a Youngest.

'Where from?' I ask, aware that my questions are irritating them but asking them anyway.

'The nutrition plant,' they reply, nodding towards a large square building at the top of the meadow. It's painted the same colour as the sky, rendering it almost invisible on a day like this. A thin trail of white smoke is snaking out of a stubby chimney at one end of the roof. Directly below it is a door bearing a bright emblem that I don't recognise. Its colours match the plantation in front of it, another clever act of disguise.

'Where does the nutrition come from? Vegetation wastage?'

Ritch-U doesn't reply.

'It's an impressive building,' I continue. 'I'm guessing the Guru didn't build it themself. Must have been here when the Settlers arrived, I suppose?'

'I don't know.' They are clearly uninterested.

'The Island was inhabited before?' I conjecture.

'No, it wasn't,' they say, gesturing towards a small circular platform at the edge of the diamond. 'You stand there.'

They walk purposefully along the neat walkway at the edge of the meadow towards an identical platform at the other end, by the nutrition plant. I take my place. The varied scents of the vegetation rows mingle to create an intoxicating bouquet that teases my taste buds. Just as I became aware of the gripp flower's sentience back in the Wildland with Coell-J, I finally recognise the whispering that has been an omnipresent, almost intangible background noise since we emerged from the Sanctuary: it's coming from the vegetation. From the soil. From the breeze, even. I remember Addh-C's assertion that *nothing is inanimate on a molecular level* and before Ritch-U has even reached their platform, I know what I'm expected to do. What the vegetation *wants* me to do.

I stare upwards, focussing my attention on one of the moisture clouds. With as little effort as it took to rebuff Addh-C's challenge with the boulder, I invite the cloud to move towards the meadow. It obliges. I invite it to release its moisture onto the vegetation. It does so, happily.

We were supposed to be doing that together! Ritch-U thoughtshares haughtily.

Sorry, I reply, inwardly rather pleased that I managed it without their tuition.

The cloud has deposited its load now and is dissipating, leaving its recipients shuddering with gratitude. Ritch-U indicates another with mind and we draw it over to an area of the meadow as yet unwatered. Together we create rain. But there is little joy in our mutual act, unlike the thrill of satisfaction I felt when I cast Addh-C's boulder aside or the illicit joy of those first times with Coell-J. No fragment of memory shared this time, just the clean act of watering vegetation. I feel no connection whatsoever with Ritch-U. Perhaps that's the aim of the practice.

Well done, they thoughtshare as the second cloud dissolves and the vegetation sings its approval. Then my fingers begin to tingle with a fresh burst of energy. A memory that isn't mine flashes into my mind: a ferocious storm exploding over a different, darkened growth meadow. Lightning illuminates an untidy muddle of gripp flowers, soaked by rain. Another memory springs up: gripp pollen bursts into another burst of light, Youngest laughter echoing across the suncycles.

These are Addh-C's memories.

The sky explodes above us, and a dancing cloud empties itself onto a startled Ritch-U. Addh-C and I laugh. Then another moisture cloud drenches me. Addh-C and I laugh harder. Though I can't see them, I know which bulderbramble bush is concealing them. With a playful flick of my mind, I grab a moisture cloud and empty it onto the bush. There is a joyous yelp. Addh-C steps out from their hiding place, soaking wet.

Ritch-U shoots us both an angry look and leaves the meadow. We laugh at the furious slosh of their footsteps in the mud.

'We might not be able to kill each other,' I splutter, 'but we can soak each other all right!'

We laugh. Openly. Without fear of recrimination.

32: Earth

Friday 23rd October, 2009

Checking first that they couldn't be overheard, Carol asked, 'What's really going on here, Andy?'

Andy wiped his mouth with his hand before speaking quietly and grimly:

'We've seen it all from the Nook. They ship a van-full in—protestors, immigrants, the homeless—and dump them here in the school, or sometimes in the leisure centre. Then they make it easy for them; doors left *accidentally* un-padlocked, windows ajar; they let them believe they've managed to escape by themselves. Then one by one they're dragged underground and eaten. Problem solved, clean hands.'

'What problem, though?' Carol asked, appalled. 'Who's responsible for all this?'

'The Minister for Housing,' Andy replied. 'Didn't you hear their election manifesto? *We'll make Britain Great again, we'll close the borders, take the homeless off the streets, give homes and work to everyone who deserves them by being born here.* Yeah right!'

'They are building more homes though!' Robert protested. 'Thousands of them!'

'And half of those are second homes,' Johnny said from the floor, 'for them that want to take a nice little holiday from the cities whilst the builders are in! There's nothing like the end of the world to provide opportunities for the rich to get richer and the poor to be exploited and blamed for everything! Because of course nothing's ever *their* fault, is it? It's not their fault we couldn't get non-existent work to pay our bills when the world economy crashed, and surely it's obvious that *we* were the ones that let the bug-eyed monsters invade, not to mention…. Oh, forget it,

Bobby. You bury your head in the sand like a good little ostrich and let the big boys do all the work.'

Robert looked at Carol helplessly.

I think he might be more upset about Stevie than he's letting on, she telepathed. *I wouldn't take it personally.*

Robert nodded sadly, recalling Johnny's infamous schooldays tantrums, which once upon a time he'd be able to puncture with a joke or a friendly hug. Not anymore.

'You're quite an orator, young man. I could use you on my team when we get out of this.'

Bridget Crowley was standing over Johnny holding a bent chair leg in her left hand. He scrambled to his feet.

'I hate to disillusion you,' he said, 'but the only way we're going to get out of this is by eating each other and making a tank out of broken chairs! Oh! I see you've made a start!'

She paused, then laughed.

'Humour in the face of diversity! I like it! You're definitely welcome on my side of the House—once they've rebuilt it, that is!'

Johnny cracked an uneasy smile.

'Done it!' the woman in fatigues called over from a window, which she'd managed to prise open.

'Well done, Sue,' Crowley smiled across, then addressed the classroom:

'All right, ladies and gentlemen, here's the plan. Susan spotted a couple of trucks parked the other side of the school playground when we were brought in from the van. We're going to steal them and get the hell out of here!'

A buzz of excitement filled the room.

'I'm sorry, Miss Crowley,' Andy announced, 'but that won't work. Those trucks are dummies, we've already checked them out—no engines.'

Crowley looked suspicious.

'There is another possibility,' Carol suggested. 'There's some equipment over in the pub that'll help us escape. If you let Robert and I go first, we can fetch it for you, without endangering anyone.'

'Do you think we're stupid?' the boy with the scabs sneered. 'You two go first and steal the trucks, leaving us here to rot. Screw that!'

With that, he pushed his way through the crowd that had gathered by the window and, with an athletic leap, launched himself out of the room. This precipitated a small riot, everyone fighting each other for a chance to escape, despite Crowley's calls for order.

Robert and Carol made a decision, told Andy and Johnny to stay in the classroom and jaunted across to the Devil's Nook. Once inside, they worked together to pull one of the tables away from the window, just in time to see the playground burst open beneath scab boy and swallow him up.

33: Barr-Byzhan

Dagre-Math, Sennith 2/7, Suncycle Exhih

After the incident in the growth meadow, Ritch-U refuses to train with me, and I end up spending most of my time with Addh-C. They're a good teacher and I pride myself on being a better pupil to them than I would ever have been with Ritch-U. It's not long before I can thoughtshare in more than the simplest of sentences. Together we perfect the art of object manipulation to the point where random memories no longer intrude. Those we share on our own terms, learning about each other's lives in such intimate detail that I feel I lived Addh-C's younghood with them. There are some memories that they don't share, saying that certain experiences are 'reserved for the Guru's assessment'. I come to resent Clahh-M's hold on Addh-C, never quite able to abandon my initial distrust, though I recognise that that might be due in part to my experiences with the Friar.

As the senniths, then moon-cycles, pass, I occasionally wonder about my Designators. Even if my Primary were disinterested in my whereabouts, surely my Secondary would have made discreet enquiries about me, in that sweetly understated way of theirs? Addh-C tries to persuade me that the majority of Designators accept our disappearance with indifference, rather than risk being publicly linked to the Not Like. If this is true, it's disturbing. But there's no way, I think, that mine could possibly know I was a Sup. When they last saw me, I was about to be pairbonded, after all.

Barram-L! I guiltily realise that I haven't even given them a thought. But then I suspect they would hardly have been heartbroken by my disappearance.

The longer I spend on the Island, the less I consider my old life. This new, haphazard way of living, where emotion takes priority over discipline and order, is my 'normal' now. A suncycle later my skin has darkened from a daily exposure to the sunlight, my hair has grown, both sets of genitalia have started to develop, maturing at an alarming rate, and I've nearly forgotten that I even had a life before Addh-C.

And then there's you. I nearly forgot about you. It's obvious that you're Not Like—how else could you be thoughtsharing?—though why only I should hear you perplexes me.

Who are you?

34: Earth

Friday 23rd October, 2009

Crowley, who'd been helping people climb down from the forced window, shouted a command as soon as she'd realised what was happening:

'The ground's unstable! Nobody move!'

But it was too late for three of the escapees, who'd been sucked into the ground already, and by the time one of them was able to reach the first van and discover that Andy had been telling the truth, two more had gone.

Carol watched helplessly from the bar. Robert, who'd been searching in vain for his backpack, shouted, 'It's not here! They must have taken it when they Tasered us!'

TIM, he telepathed, *Bring us back to the lab. We need more teleport belts! TIM?*

There was no answer.

Carol, her eyes watery with tears, looked across at him.

TIM's reboot! Robert, we—

But Robert had already jaunted back to the classroom, where the hand he offered to a young woman clambering through the window was met with a cold stare.

35: Barr-Byzhan

Dagre-Lunh, Sennith 2/ 8, Suncycle Exhih

Although my instinct tells me to keep your existence to myself, I can't help but talk about you to Addh-C, eventually. They are far less puzzled than I am, saying:

'It's going to happen more and more, as we get closer to the Final Upgrade. Everyone will reach out to someone; this Sup, whoever they are, has chosen you. Just as you chose me.'

I stop working. Addh-C doesn't. We've been assigned to shore up the walls of the same passageway we walked along a suncycle ago, having spent most of the hot season rejuvenating the soil in the burnt gripp field at its end. It's a task that would have taken hardly any time at all had we used object manipulation. But we have learnt to use our powers sparingly—not only do they tire us, they sometimes strip the tasks of any meaning or enjoyment. We've both come to cherish the sensation of soil under our fingernails and muscles that ache because they've been put to good use. We've come to appreciate a lifestyle that we would never have experienced had we become Citizens, despite it being one that we have no need to adopt as Not Like, given our powers.

'I didn't choose you,' I mouthspeak.

Yes you did.

Addh-C's focus remains on a fissure in the rock that they're spooning a chemical binder into with a small stick, picked from the remains of the burnt gripp crops a while ago and fashioned into an instrument ('my little faithful').

How do you suppose I knew your name, Daghu-N? they continue, that irritating but captivating smile playing on their lips.

You told me how, I respond. *From the chip embedded in my skull. Clahh-M downloaded my details as soon as I arrived on the Island.*

Not as soon as you arrived on the Island, Addh-C corrects me. *As soon as you arrived in the Sanctuary. Remember that dizzy spell you had? You told me your name **before** that, the moment you woke up on the beach. You chose me, Daghu-N, whether you like it or not.*

133

I do not like it. Nor do I believe it. I suspect that Addh-C has fallen for another of the Guru's fictions. For a start, it makes no sense for the cult to have waited to disable my MCL. If the chip tracked my movements, surely that would have led the authorities directly to the Sanctuary as soon as I arrived?

'We should pairbond,' Addh says suddenly, looking up from their work.

I'd laugh if the idea weren't so unthinkable.

'Not Like don't pairbond,' I state blankly.

'Who says so?' they reply.

They always sound like they're mocking me.

'*Everyone* says so,' I say. 'It's just a fact of life… Besides…'

I hesitate. We've never talked about the obvious. I've never felt able to broach the subject.

Besides…?

'Even if I wanted to—which I don't—we… couldn't. Well, *you* couldn't.'

Why not?

Don't make me say it, I think, whilst shielding my thoughts. They sense what I'm doing and, with barely any effort, reach around my mental barrier to retrieve an image. They frown.

Why should that stop us? they ask, apparently not realising the obvious. Sometimes Addh-C is like a

Youngest. Little wonder that Clahh-M finds it so easy to fool them into believing their stories.

'Because we need to make a choice, Addh-C. Primary or Secondary. It's natural. And you... I don't really understand *how*... but you...'

'I haven't been mutilated in the name of Citizenship,' Addh-C says starkly.

Once again, I don't understand. I ask them to explain. What they say beggars belief:

'The *choice* we're forced to make when we pairbond isn't *natural*, Daghu-N, far from it. *This* is natural.'

They gesture towards their genitalia, then continue, 'All Byzhans are born with the ability to develop Primary and Secondary genitalia. The surgery that the Establishment says is necessary to promote the growth of one or the other is cruel and unnatural. In fact, it's an obscenity. None of us on the Island have had it. Nor will we ever.'

I almost pity them and start to wonder whether Clahh-M's outrageous theories are in fact motivated by a warped sense of compassion. Before I can compose a rational but kind answer to the lie, there is a sharp crack from above us, followed by a shower of dust. Our careful work hasn't been enough to shore up the wall. With a massive howl of rock against rock, it crashes to the ground...

...But we aren't there.

There was music. I heard music—that same discordant mess of notes. And now our bodies are entwined, hearts pounding as one. Addh-C's breath is heavy, rasping, close to my ear. The air is still warm here, wherever this is, but more humid. Our sweat mingles. Our lips touch.

We are alive.

36: Earth

Friday 23rd October, 2009

An hour or so later, Johnny was thrust into the make-do cell that had once been a stationery cupboard. The door slammed shut behind him. Carol had been separated from the others and was now tied to one of the tiny chairs in the classroom, relaying developments telepathically to Robert, who sat glowering on a dusty stool in the corner of the cupboard.

'That's bloody perfect, that is!' Johnny said, smoothing his fatigues down.

'Well?' Andy snapped, furious that he'd been imprisoned by association with his former school friend. 'What did they say?'

'They said they won't harm her as long as Mr Spaceboy here doesn't do his disappearing trick again. If he does, then she's dead, to be blunt.'

'This is *ridiculous*!' Robert blurted out. 'How can they possibly think we were responsible for all that?! We offered to help, for heaven's sake!'

'Are you a complete idiot?' Johnny shouted back at him, 'Of *course* they think you did it! We all saw you vanish into thin air—just like the killer pixies did when they invaded! You can't expect them to just sit back and wait for the next time you try to kill them off! If it were up to Crowley, we'd all be dead already—she was all for letting the mob beat our brains out, until I suggested... Not that that made any difference, they still think I'm one of you lot. Which really pisses me off, incidentally.'

'Until you suggested *what*, Johnny?' Andy asked, provoking a nonchalant shrug from his friend, who was distracting himself with random bits of stationery. '*Johnny....*'

Before he could answer, the door was unlocked, opened and a surly man with tattoos and an XTC T-shirt pulled Johnny to his feet.

'What now?' he moaned.

'The blonde bird wants some company!' Tattoos replied with an ugly grin.

'You what?!' Johnny protested as the door slammed behind them again. The key turned in the lock.

Andy sat on a large box of photocopier paper deflatedly.

'Why's he so rude to me?' Robert complained, 'I don't get it!'

'Of course you don't,' Andy shook his head. 'You never did.'

'Eh?'

Andy closed his eyes wearily.

Robert! Carol telepathed, *They're planning on sending me out into the playground. It was Johnny's idea—if I fall through the asphalt, they'll know where not to go when they try to get to the second van! They're convinced that one's going to work!*

That was Johnny's idea? Robert responded, confused.

Perhaps he thought I could jaunt out when the floor opens up, she suggested charitably, *which I probably could do if I'm quick enough. But now they're making him come with me! We have to do something—we can't let the creature get to him!*

Robert stood up and focussed on the door. After a series of small clunks, the lock sprung open.

'Stay here!' Robert told Andy, opening the door and walking into the classroom.

As he did, he felt his stomach churn again, saw his skin erupt with the same blue energy as before.

Not again, please not now!! Carol, jaunt!! Go!!

Carol was being untied by Susan, Crowley's second-in-command. Johnny was being held by the window ready to be pushed out onto the playground. Robert fell to his knees, his whole body shimmering. As soon as Crowley saw him, she nodded to Tattoos, standing behind Carol. Susan stepped aside and he swung a sharp-edged chair leg above his head and then downwards… into thin air.

37: Barr-Byzhan

Dagre-Lunh, Sennith 2/9, Suncycle Exhih

If this is the Broken Hemisphere, as we assume it is, it's been misnamed. This place, far from being 'broken', is a jumbled distillation of everything that ever existed on Barr-Byzhan; everything, that is, except the Byzhans themselves. Every plant, every animal shares this wildland, a maelstrom of colours, sounds, smells, unlike anything either of us could ever comprehend. Only one suncycle ago, this would have terrified me—ruefully I recall that first encounter with the untampered wildland in the

Citadel (a sorry imitation of this magnificent place) and my fear of the unfamiliar birdsong on the Island. But I feel safe here, protected somehow. Already, Addh-C has met and been nuzzled by the wild shortnecks. We've tasted the joy of buzzing insects as they feast on the pollen of uncultivated gripp flowers. We've sipped from a stream that bursts from a hole in an uneven sedoposs wall, polished into blackstone by the icy water as it cascades into a curving gully in the wildland floor. We've allowed every creature to examine our thoughts, find no desire to harm them and wander away without confrontation.

We've found only one sign of civilisation here: a small hut, old, embraced by the Wildland, whose tendrils have pierced the roof and walls and found a new place to shelter from the sunlight. Constructed from an unnatural combination of wood and metal (Addh-C laughs as I pronounce it so, but old habits die hard), it shows no signs of purpose or inhabitation. When we first discover it, it stinks; a dead shortneck decays in the corner; my first encounter with death. Overcome with nausea and sorrow, we bury the corpse in a clearing not far from the hut, which we then adopt as our temporary home. It's only when Addh-C starts to tear away dead vegetation from the walls that we discover a fading emblem, colours muted by age. Neither of us recognise it at first. Then, later, when we've been laughing at the memory of Ritch-U being drenched in the growth meadow, I make the connection: it's the same emblem that is painted on the door of the nutrition plant on the Island. We wonder about the significance of the connection for a little while, but our focus lies on our existence in this new place, wherever it is.

'Why this obsession with gripp smokes?' I ask Addh-C the following cycle as they gather the plants they've picked and carefully separate petals from stems. 'Apart from them being a Nikey thing.'

'Have you never *tried* one?' they ask, not even looking up.

I shake my head. I toy with telling them about the Friar's infusion, but decide against it.

'My Primary used to smoke them,' I explain. 'I hated the smell.'

'I bet your Primary never smoked the real thing! Those manufactured smokes were mostly chemicals, probably never even been close to gripp pollen, just crushed petals. That's what gave them the awful smell.'

'What's important about the pollen?'

'It's the gripp pollen that relaxes you—or rather, the pollen's interaction with the catalyst in your blood.'

'I don't understand.'

Addh-C gives me one of their looks; the one that says *I pity you,* but also, *that's so sweet.*

Just tell me how it works, I thoughtshare impatiently.

Addh-C holds up a petal and shakes it gently. There's a delicate shower of pollen.

Gripp pollen. You breathe it in. It gets into your bloodstream through the lungs. It searches for the pleasure enzyme in your blood. When they find each other, WHAM! The pollen eats the enzyme and then shares the pleasure with you. It's a very generous pollen.

'And what if you don't have the enzyme?'

'Everyone has the enzyme.'

Addh-C holds up a concoction of leaf, petal and pollen that bears only the slightest resemblance to a smoke.

'Let's try one.'

'No thank you,' I reply haughtily.

They've already lit it and are sucking in its fumes. Their expression changes to one of enviable gratification. I pretend not to be curious but they know me too well.

Come here.

They pull me towards them and touch my mouth with theirs. Our breath mingles. I taste gripp smoke for the first time. And I understand why Addh-C has been missing it. It has a similar effect to the Friar's infusion, but the feelings it evokes in me are far, far more intense. Though maybe that's more to do with whom I'm sharing it with than the smoke itself. That dark-cyc we sleep like Youngests. The following cycle, I pick a feverfruit straight from the tree and the juice is sharp, intense, delicious. Addh-C licks it from my chin, a provocatively intimate act. We giggle like Youngests.

We should pairbond and stay here forever, they pronounce.

The idea is so absurd that we laugh even more. I twist my body round and rest my head on their chest, gazing up through the rippling canopy to the matte green sky.

So how did you do it?

Do what?

Placeroam. Did you just picture this and then make it happen? How does it work?

I don't know how it works, Addh-C. I don't even know if it was me that made it happen.

*Of course it was! You're the only one who **can** do it, Daghu-N. You saved our lives.*

I saved our lives? Is that possible? If it really was me that brought us here, I have no idea how we're supposed to get *back* to the Sanctuary. Though we've established that we're in no immediate danger from the wildlife, how long can we survive on feverfruit and gripp-smokes? How far are we from civilisation? If this is the Broken Hemisphere, then the only Byzhans we're likely to meet will be little more than savages. They'll be far more inclined to kill us than the animals. No Citizen has ever returned from the Broken Hemisphere alive; what makes us more likely to survive than anyone else?

Are *you* here somewhere? Did you bring us here? If you did, where are you hiding? Why haven't you shown yourself? Maybe you can't. Maybe this is a trap. Maybe you were ensnared first and they're forcing you to thoughtshare with me, whoever they are, and now we're going to be trapped too.

A shudder of fear runs through me. Addh-C strokes my hair gently, an attempt to pacify me. But the demons are starting to take hold.

'In one of the Catharsae,' I say, 'an air transport vehicle crash-landed in the Broken Hemisphere and the crew ended up eating each other to survive!'

Stories, Addh-C thoughtshares, yawning.

'Why should the real thing be any different?' I react, pulling myself out of their embrace and standing. I walk across to the open doorway. The wildland seems

144

to go on forever, the leaves and branches thicker and darker the further away they are, on all sides.

'As long as I get to eat you first…' Addh-C mouthspeaks, closing their eyes with a lazy smile.

'Is everything a wittical to you?' I snap. 'For The Creator's sake, Addh-C, we nearly died back on the Island! And we might never get back if I can't work out how to… Oh no! *Don't you dare!!'*

But it's too late. Addh-C has opened their mind to me and their memories and feelings are cascading over me, an intoxicating balm, one that they've learnt to use when I've woken from nightmares in the middle of the dark-cyc, or been crippled by anxiety in the cyclelight.

It's even better than gripp-smoke and it always works.

I'm carried away on a warm fragment of their past, cossetted by their carefree optimism, and eventually, as always, I wonder what it was that made me so anxious to begin with. *Of course* we can stay here. *Of course* we can survive. *Of course* we can pairbond… I lie down and give in to Addh-C's embrace again.

Nottagh-N, please not now!! Carr-L jaunt!! Go!!

Your words slice through the calm of our sleep, turning my blood cold, slapping me awake. Addh-C has rolled over to face away from me, their bare back familiar in the dappled moonlight. I clutch them to me, terrified, just as the music begins and the blinding wave of energy hits us.

38: Earth

Friday 23rd October, 2009

It took a moment or two for Carol's eyes to adjust to the darkness. As she hadn't had time to touch her belt, she had no idea where she'd jaunted to, but wherever it was, the air was cold, damp and smelt of decaying flesh. A shifting of muscles and skin to her right made her shudder. The creature must be down here, and it seemed close. There was another shift to her left. And then behind her.

Carol blinked as she started to make out shapes in the dark. There were at least six of them, moving slowly towards her.

She was surrounded.

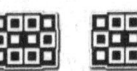

39: Barr-Byzhan

'So, you and Addh-C wish to pairbond?'

Clahh-M has summoned me to their work chamber. Their tone is indecipherable, their expression calm. I can't tell whether they disapprove or not.

'Addh-C wants to,' I venture. 'But we can't, can we?'

They nod slowly.

'It is illegal for Not Likes to pairbond,' they say, 'but not unheard of. When the Final Upgrade happens, the concept will be up for discussion, along with every aspect of the law. And, as you must have realised already, we don't abide by the Establishment's rules here on the Island.'

They smile, but it's a thin smile lacking warmth. I wonder if the Guru is worried that their most devout follower will be distracted from their devotion if we pairbond.

'I know that Addh-C would never do it if you were to disapprove,' I lie, thinking of the times they've tried to persuade me to take us both back to the Broken Hemisphere, lest Clahh-M doesn't give us their blessing. Already we've lied to our fellow Islanders, explaining our cycles away from the Sanctuary as a fruitless exploration of the uncharted parts of the Island. Immediately I shield my thoughts (a trick Addh-C and I developed after Ritch-U accused us of thoughtsharing in the Eating Hall) but Clahh-M shows no sign of having read my mind. Theirs is, as ever, unreadable.

'How could I disapprove?' they reply. 'You and Addh-C are a perfect couple… Ideal, in fact.'

Their compliment—if it is one—sounds like an afterthought, albeit a strangely loaded one. Clahh-M crosses the chamber and stops at a large cabinet which has been crudely hand-painted. I recognise the style, if not the subject matter. They obviously entrusted their most devout follower with the decoration. They unlock the cabinet door, which swings open. This seems like an odd action and it's only later that I realise it's because Clahh-M has used a key to do it. The Not Like don't need keys. At the time, though, I'm distracted by the cabinet's contents, and—in particular—my Primary's gold pin. It's been polished since I saw it last and sits at the gleaming centre of a neatly ordered collection of jewellery. I'm reminded of the display case of holy artefacts at the Temple of the West Pyramids. I wonder whom the other pieces of jewellery belong to. Is it possible that Clahh-M has gathered together a collection of trophies from each of his followers? Surely not. There are well over a hundred pieces.

They close and lock the cabinet door again, pocketing the key with one hand and holding out a shiny chain in the other.

'My pairbonding gift to you,' they smile, genuinely this time. 'Be sure to wear it at all times, it will bring great blessings to your union.'

They indicate that I should turn round so that they can place it around my neck. I do so, thanking them. The chain is heavy, the metal cool to the touch. Showing no signs of intimacy (Addh-C would have made me tremble with the same movements), Clahh-M lifts the medallion at the end of the chain and drops it inside my shirt. Unlike the necklace, the medallion is light, insubstantial. I recognise its design from somewhere—a Clerical symbol maybe? Something from the Ancient times?

Though Addh-C is delighted that the Guru has given us their blessing, they seem less enamoured of the necklace itself. I suspect it's because Clahh-M chose to give it to me rather than to them and suggest as much when it's time to retire for the dark-cyc. Addh-C dismisses the idea with obvious irritation, which provokes me into keeping it on when I've taken everything else off. I glance at the medallion as I walk provocatively towards them and suddenly realise where I've seen it before: it's the same as the one that Coell-J was wearing in the Wildland back when we were Youngers. And at its bottom edge, just below the symbol of ancient fertility, is a tiny crack.

40: Earth

Friday 23rd October, 2009

A series of quick jaunts, enabled by the 'safe return' button on her belt, had led Carol back to the Lab, where TIM was silent, the lights were low and Robert was sitting, lost in thought. He'd laid a pile of teleport belts on the circular table below TIM's darkened spheres and was absentmindedly fiddling with one of the buckles.

Carol stepped off the jaunting pad and walked over to sit by him.

'Are you okay?' she asked.

'I think so,' he nodded. 'It didn't last as long this time. It's all a bit… random. But the fact that it's only happening to *me*, and it doesn't seem to matter where I am… Surely that means… something…'

He trailed off, aware that Carol was probably less inclined than he was to believe that his dead boyfriend was not only alive but trying to reach him through a fragment of time-space corridor.

'Do you think that's wise?' she asked, nodding towards the belts.

'I don't know,' Robert replied. 'They want to kill us, but if we don't get them out of there…'

'They'll die,' Carol said bluntly. 'If TIM were online, he could programme their belts to take them to a place of safety, not here. But I haven't got the technical ability to do that.'

'Me neither.'

'And if they come here, who knows what damage they might do? Even letting Bridget Crowley see the Lab might be dangerous. She's a political opportunist. Freedom Party or not, she wants to be in power, and access to Federation technology might… well, we mustn't risk it.'

'So, we just let that creature kill Andy, Johnny and the others?' Robert asked.

'That's another thing,' said Carol. 'There's more than one creature. I jaunted down into one of the tunnels, right into what felt like some sort of nest. There could be *hundreds* of them underneath Barcombe Hill.'

'Then we've *got* to go back!' Robert exclaimed, standing.

'I'm sorry, Robert, but we can't do that. We have to wait for TIM to finish his reboot. Then we'll have more control over the situation, and we can really help those people without endangering ourselves.'

'How long's that going to be?' Robert asked, exasperated.

'I don't know,' Carol replied, reaching out her hand to lay it on his. 'Not long, I'm sure. We must be patient, Robert.'

41: Barr-Byzhan

Dagre-Laugh, Sennith 2/9, Suncycle Exhih

My illness comes on that night. My dreams are especially tortuous: Coell-J accuses me of stealing their medallion, of betraying them to the authorities; Addh-C spurns me for their Guru and I am forced to conduct the pairbonding ceremony myself; my Primary interrupts the ceremony to declare it immoral and sacrifices my Secondary to The Creator as an act of penitence on my behalf; I wake with the sharp tang of their blood in my nostrils, my ears ringing still with their screams.

The chamber seems darker than it should be. Addh-C is saying something to me, but I can only catch the odd word. I try to reach out to them, but my arms feel numb and powerless. Addh-C is thoughtsharing now, but I can hear nothing. Nor can I reply. The necklace weighs heavily on my chest but is cold: a welcome relief from the unbearable heat of the chamber. Addh-C is stroking my hair tenderly, but their touch sends shards of pain searing through me. I shake them off and pass out again.

I don't know how long I'm unconscious but when I wake again, I feel even weaker. The chamber is darker, and I can barely open my eyes.

'Is it the Madness?'

Addh-C's voice. I'm flushed with fear. Am I dying?

'They haven't shown any other symptoms,' Clahh-M replies in the darkness, 'but we should probably isolate them in case.'

Please don't let me die alone.

'I'm not leaving them.'

'You'd risk contamination?'

There is no reply. I can't tell how long the silence lasts; time has started to lose its meaning in this terrible new reality. I'm not sure how long I've been ill, even. Was I ill back in the monastery? Or in that other place, the one with the shortnecks and the icy water? Is that what poisoned me? Is that why I'm dying?

Yes, I hear Coell-J say, *we poisoned you because you're a Nikey and deserve to die. You and your half-Dravvhan freak!*

'I'd risk anything, Guru.'

The Freak is talking.

'Then we'll have to isolate you as well, Addh-C. I'm sorry. But if it *is* the Madness…'

'I understand.'

I don't.

I don't understand anything anymore.

42: Earth

Saturday 24th October, 2009

It was dawn when Johnny came to. Way above him, the warm, orange rays of the rising sun smeared light onto the edges of the hole that had opened up beneath him only yards away from the second van. Seconds before he'd fallen, he'd heard a cry, turned and watched Andy being swallowed up behind him. Just like Stevie.

All those years ago, he'd never imagined that they'd know each other their whole lives, never imagined that they'd die together, here in the very place they'd met. He never imagined that he'd witness the terror in his friends' eyes as they screamed Johnny's name, begging him to save them. Never imagined the hollow feeling in his guts when his own end came; the awful certainty that, as he fell, this breath would be his last.

And yet it hadn't been. By some insane quirk of fate, his fall had been broken by—what? Something covered with a rough matting that gave way a little as he pulled himself up to his feet. Was he standing on a pile of sand? It reeked of manure. Something down here was definitely rotting. Maybe the matting was covering a pile of corpses. Was this place the creature's larder? Johnny's stomach turned at the memory of its monstrous face glaring up at him from Stevie's corpse, yellow eyes glistening in the torchlight, vicious fangs dripping with blood. Then an older memory flashed into his head: Bobby grasping him as an adder slithered out from beneath a sheet of corrugated iron somewhere in Cornwall. Their mutual revulsion and fascination as they watched it slink off into the bracken. The teasing and laughter on the beach afterwards: 'You screamed like a Nelly!' 'I did not! *You* were the one that screamed!'

They'd been children. Now Robert Mitchell was some sort of freak, probably miles away, and Johnny was stuck underground clambering over a pile of dead people. He scrabbled around at his feet for his torch but found nothing.

'Well, that's bloody perfect, that is!' he spat, then cursed again as he tripped on something hard poking out of the pile, landing head first in the matting beyond it.

As he fell, the matting split and his face was splattered with foul-smelling liquid. Disgusted, he immediately retched violently.

'Johnny?'

A white beam illuminated the messy mound in front of him. He realised with horror that he'd fallen into a huge, dead, alien eye.

43: Barr-Byzhan

Dagre-Frigh, Sennith 3/ 1, Suncycle Exhih

Another feverish dream: Coell-J again. This time, they're caught up in the bulderbramble bush in the Courtyard, only the leaves aren't pink, they're blood red. Its branches and tendrils wrap themselves around Coell-J's body, thorns piercing their skin, their scarlet blood darkening the leaves even further. I try to pull the twisted vegetation away from Coell-J, but this only makes them tighten their grip.

I deserve to die, Daghu-N! Coell-J screams, their eyes wide, terrified. *Let me go! Let the bulderbramble take me!*

Powerless, I watch the bush crush them into pulp and devour them. The old rhyme hangs mockingly in the air, chanted by whom? Addh-C? Clahh-M? No, the voice is cruel, cold. My Primary? Friar Coen? No.

Hatch-G-Mah. It's the Establishmentor themself, taunting me in my dreams.

Finally, some cycles later, I wake without the darkness and the sheen of sweat. My limbs feel as heavy as they did before, but I can focus on the chamber now. An untouched tray of food has been left in the corridor outside. An insect buzzes around it, no doubt glad of the pickings. I listen to the grateful fluttering of its wings and try to focus on its joy but feel and hear none.

My stomach burns with hunger. I turn my head to see Addh-C lying on the bed beside me. I can tell immediately that they're as ill as I am. They're also naked, aside from a necklace made from the same heavy metal as mine. At the end of it is a small, colourful feather, bound to the chain with rough thread. With effort, I reach over and stroke the feather.

Addh-C, who has been staring at the ceiling, starts.

It's only me, I thoughtshare… or try to.

'It didn't work,' Addh-C whispers, their voice hoarse with fever.

'What didn't?' I ask, my voice also cracked.

'The Guru's charm,' they reply. 'It was supposed to protect me from the Madness.'

'Of *course* it didn't work!' I snap, then my blood turns cold again. 'Is that what we've got, then? The Madness? Oh Creator, are we dying?'

'At least we won't be doing it alone,' Addh-C sighs, closing their eyes.

'So, is that it, then?!' I say, irritated by their uncharacteristic pessimism. 'We just roll over and die? What's wrong with you, Addh-C?'

'I'm *dying*, Daghu-N,' they reply bitterly. 'It's already taken our powers, who knows what's next? Our sanity?'

So that's why I can't thoughtshare.

'I can't believe that Clahh-M would just let us die,' I mutter, then, overwhelmed with tiredness, close my eyes. 'Oh, maybe I can. They never liked me. You should've seen them when I said you were the one who wanted to pairbond. It wouldn't surprise me if they'd deliberately infected me with the Madness to get me out of the way!'

'How dare you say that?!' Addh-C spits. 'After all they've done for us? The Guru's *devoted* to us, to the Sanctuary. If anything, we're their *favourites*. They said as much when I told them about the placeroaming.'

'You told Clahh-M about it?'

'I know we agreed not to, but I thought they should know.' They shrug. 'You're wrong about the Guru, Daghu-N. Just look at what they achieved in one suncycle! Why would they do that if… if… You're delusional. It must be the Madness talking.'

'*Is* this the Madness, though?' My mind is racing. 'Neither of us had any of the symptoms—the rash, the memory loss, the lack of appetite—in fact, I'm ravenous…'

Suddenly I start to realise what my dreams have been telling me.

'The bulderbramble bushes!' I gasp, heaving myself into a sitting position, head spinning. 'Addh-C, you said they planted them in the Courtyard when they arrived, a suncycle ago!'

'So?'

159

'They didn't! The leaves are pink. They've been there for at least four suncycles. They lied to us!'

In the distance, there's the ominous drone of a transportation engine.

'So, the bushes have been here for longer than a suncycle!' Addh-C replies. 'What does it matter?'

'Why would Clahh-M lie about that if they weren't trying to hide something? I don't trust them, Addh-C. I don't think that's the only thing they've been lying to us about!'

The throb of engines grows louder and closer. There's more than one of them.

'The growth meadows!' I continue. 'They're out in the open—easily visible from the air!'

'So?'

'So why haven't they been spotted before now?'

'Even if they had been, they wouldn't mean anything to anyone—it's all vegetation, nothing that wouldn't grow here naturally.'

'But the growth meadow *isn't* natural!'

The tone of the engines changes; they're manoeuvring into position above the Island.

'We both know that, Addh-C!' I say, breathless with the realisation. 'It seems *natural* to anyone who's grown up on the Mainland, where *nature* is as tempered as its Citizens are, but it's not! *Real* wildland is *messy,* and all the better for it! The growth meadows are a target!'

The chamber is rocked by the first explosion.

'Your Guru's led them here, Addh-C!' I exclaim. 'They've betrayed us! I don't think they're even Not Like! They forbade us to thoughtshare because they can't do it themselves!'

'Daghu-N!' Addh-C has tears in their eyes. 'What's happened to you? Is it the Madness?'

Another explosion, closer.

'It's all lies, Addh-C!' I rip the chain from my neck and brandish it at them. 'This medallion belonged to the first Sup I knew—how did it end up in Clahh-M's work chamber?!'

My body suddenly feels stronger, my head clearer. Only the hand holding the chain remains numb. I let it fall to the floor. A crack of gunfire echoes down the corridor, followed by footsteps. Clahh-M runs into the chamber, gun in hand.

Take the chain off, Addh-C! I urge them, but they don't hear me.

The Guru raises their gun to fire.

44: Earth

'What is he, then? A pixie agent? Some sort of genetic experiment?'

Johnny and Andy were huddled in a tunnel about ten feet away from the dead animal they'd both fallen onto from the playground. After a few attempts to climb up one of the holes, they'd given up; any gaps in the rock that might have served as footholds were too far apart, and the surface was curiously smooth otherwise. At least here, where the tunnel ended, they'd be able to see their monstrous executioner when it approached them, thanks to the torch that Andy had found nestling in the dead beast's belly. And there was a possibility that together they might be able to fight it off before it ate them. At least that's what they were telling each other. Neither of them was actually convinced they had a hope in hell of surviving this. So, they were distracting themselves with idle conversation, which after a while predictably settled on Robert Mitchell.

'I don't know.' Andy sighed. 'When his therapist and those weirdos took us out of that place under the stones, they were going on about him having psychic

162

powers or something. Maybe the lockpicking and the teleport stuff is all part of that.'

'Oh, so he had a therapist, did he?' Johnny sneered. 'Of course he bloody did.'

'Come off it, Johnny!' Andy said wearily. 'Cut all that crap, will you?! Bobby never said anything about being *better* than us! Besides, I was an architect, you were a landscape gardener, perhaps he *is* better than us!'

'That was *before*,' Johnny growled, 'and I wasn't just talking about *jobs*, it's his whole *attitude!* And now he's got super-powers, he'll be even worse!'

'It's all in your head, Johnny.'

Andy knew better than to bring up what he believed was the real reason for his friend's anger— that he was in love with Robert, and always had been. He'd suggested that once back in the sixth form and got a black eye for it. Johnny's girlfriend—what was her name? Jess? Jenny?—got pregnant shortly afterwards, leading to a disastrous marriage that had only lasted a year. Both ex-wife and son were killed when the Tnawi blasted most of central London, leaving Johnny alone and bitter about *everything*. Andy and Stevie had been the only people he seemed to trust. Perhaps because they were the only ones who truly knew who and what Johnny Turner was?

'Did you notice?' Andy said, trying to change the subject. 'The buildings that fell into the ground, they're all old. The church, the old manor house, even the folly above the railway tunnel. All part of the original village.'

'So?'

Johnny seemed disinterested, which was better than angry.

'I just noticed, that's all. And then there's this.' He picked up the piece of wood that he'd been holding as a makeshift weapon, not that it would do much good against the creature; it was so brittle that parts of it had crumbled away as soon as he'd picked it up. 'I think it was a bit of foundation. This should be solid stone, but it isn't. It's like something's sucked part of its innards out somehow. Interesting, isn't it?'

'Not really.'

There was a brief silence, then they both laughed.

'Idiot!' Andy said, slapping his friend playfully on the arm.

They both froze as they heard what sounded like windchimes echoing down the tunnel towards them. The discordant notes only lasted a few seconds, then there was a voice:

'What on earth is *that*?'

Robert Mitchell's voice.

Andy swore he was a smile flicker across Johnny's face. Then they heard the scrabble of claws on rock, and a low growling which sharpened into a ferocious howl.

45: Barr-Byzhan

Dagre-Frigh, Sennith 3/1, Suncycle Exhih

Addh-C? Can you hear me? I've placeroamed again. I'm back in the Citadel. Addh-C, where are you?

There is no reply. Only the distant rumble of traffic.

Addh-C? Addh-C?

Nothing. It was the chains that made us ill, that robbed us of our powers, it must have been. The chains that Clahh-M insisted that we wore. But why? Could it have been that they didn't want us to placeroam? That they wanted us on the Island for whatever was about to happen when I left it? Did Clahh-M want us dead or captured, along with the other Not Like in the Sanctuary? If so, I'm now a fugitive, on the run from whoever employed them to gather us together. If they knew we were on the Island all along, then maybe the MCL in my head hasn't been disabled and they'll easily track me

165

down. My mind is racing, my heart pounding. I start to feel unsure of everything and everyone. What if Addh-C themself were part of the deception, what if everything that happened between us was a lie? The Not Like are deceivers; they have to be, to survive.

I have to hide. I have to go home.

The locks are different. Double-coded now as well as the traditional key. I pass my hand over the coder unit, which responds to my request without dispute, as does the traditional lock. I nearly collide with my Secondary, who is thinner, noticeably older. Their eyes widen as they recognise me.

'You can't be here!' they whisper, preventing me coming in any further.

'I have to, Sec-Sec!' I reply. 'I need somewhere to…'

'You *have to go!*' they hiss, pushing me back towards the door. I hear footsteps somewhere in the pod behind them. 'We know about you, Daghu-N! *Everybody knows!* You must go!'

I go. I run. I hide. For a whole suncycle, I hide in places where nobody can find me. I stowaway on sea transport ships, I roam the Wildlands and the deserts. I placeroam, maybe three or four times. It only seems to happen in moments of crisis, when I'm in danger of being recognised or arrested. It feels guttural, instinctive. I ache for Addh-C and the simplicity and warmth of their embrace. And if it's instinct that enables me to placeroam, perhaps the growing desire to find out what happened to them will suffice.

On a blazingly hot cycle in an abandoned transportation hub not far from Hoss-Well Point, I slip into the cool clerical uniform that I stole from the drying lines outside the monastery. I close my eyes and try to picture Addh-C's face.

They're smiling, warmly but with the air of mockery that I've missed. I let my mind travel down their body like a searchlight, investigating every crease in their skin, each muscle and hair; I can smell them, hear them, taste them.

I know where you are, I thoughtshare, as the notes gather in the corners of the hub, sending sparks of blue energy dancing into the air towards me, where I haul them into my mind and body, ready to leave this place…

…and stand once again on the Island.

46: Earth

Saturday 24th October, 2009

There was a flash, followed by the piercing zap of a ray gun. Andy saw the body of the alien creature illuminated mid-leap, claws raised, sharp teeth glistening between its crocodile-like jaws. Then, in the darkness, he heard the thump of its body hitting the ground. He pointed his torch, batteries dying, towards where it had fallen. At the same time, Robert emerged from behind the larger animal, light dancing from a lamp on his forehead. The older woman, Carol, was binding the creature's limbs together with gently glowing rope.

'Put these on,' Robert urged him and Johnny, handing them gaudy-looking belts with oddly shaped metal buckles, 'before any of its friends find us!'

'What do you mean by…'

Andy's question was interrupted by the appearance of another alien creature, shrieking as it raced down the tunnel towards them. Carol, who'd wrapped another belt around the one on the floor, appeared to stare blankly into the space behind them for a second. Then the windchimes sounded again, this time much louder and nearer, and the tunnel shimmered out of existence, to be replaced by... what? A small nightclub of some sort. 1970s themed, judging by the undulating, multi-coloured projections on the walls. No music; not open yet. Retro leather sofas. In the middle of the bar, a circular table, uplit, no drinks on it yet. Above it, some sort of art installation, or was it a ventilation unit? Plastic tubes emerged from it and disappeared into the walls.

'Well, that's bloody perfect, that is!'

'Give me a hand, will you, Johnny?' Carol asked, indicating the dead creature's feet.

He grabbed its legs and together they manoeuvred it onto what looked like a sun lounger in one corner of the bar.

'Forcefield please, TIM,' Carol said.

Andy glanced around the room for someone else.

'Yes, Carol,' a voice replied out of a PA somewhere above them. The ventilation unit flashed in time with the words, bizarrely.

A shimmering square blue curtain of light fizzed into life around the sun lounger. The creature twitched in response; not dead, then.

'Okay, what's going on?' Johnny demanded. 'I get the teleport bit—I've seen *Star Trek*—but why bring the killer thing here? Is it *yours*?'

'Of course not!' Robert snapped, wandering over to the creature, which was becoming increasingly agitated. 'And, as for what's going on, we've just saved you from being eaten! TIM checked for human lifesigns in Barcombe Hill and yours were the only ones. No need to thank us.'

Carol raised an admonishing eyebrow at him.

'We're the only ones left?' Andy repeated, feeling nauseous.

Carol nodded sadly, then she addressed the ventilation unit:

'TIM, there was another creature, much larger. I think it was dead. From their behaviour, I'd guess the others were trying to protect it from something. Maybe us?'

'Have you been able to identify…' Robert started, then suddenly fell to his knees, the force field buzzing angrily as his head bounced off it.

Andy moved towards him, but Carol held him back.

'TIM, is it…?'

'Yes, Carol,' the PA sounded. 'I'm registering the same disturbance as last time and triangulating the corridor's exact co-ordinates.'

There was a sudden thud and spit of electricity, as if a fuse had blown somewhere in the nightclub. The walls dimmed and the ventilation unit's lights went out completely.

'TIM?!' Carol sounded panicked.

Robert was glowing now, a bluish white haze that leapt out of him and into the creature, which was struggling against its bindings, head flicking from side to side. Andy realised with horror that the forcefield had disappeared. Carol leapt for the gun that she'd tossed aside when they'd arrived. Robert's head jerked up and, in unison with the writhing creature, yelled out:

'Mummy! I want my Mummy!'

47: Barr-Byzhan

Dagre-Sunonh, Sennith 3/0, Suncycle Eftah

I expected devastation. I expected the growth meadow to be back in its infancy, if anything, small sprouts of vegetation rising from charred soil. But

171

the diamond is alive with colour, the plants thriving, bearing healthy fruit. Behind me, the nutrition plant hums gently, sending regular bursts of liquid through the pipes and into the soil. Not far away from me, a worker, barely more than a Youngest, is standing holding a pair of clippers in one hand and freshly harvested feverfruit in the other. They're staring at something behind me, their mouth open slightly. Is there something wrong with the nutrition plant? I glance back at it and then realise that of course the Younger is staring at me.

Hello, I thoughtshare, wondering as I do whether they're a Sup or not. Their mouth widens further.

Hello, they reply, then blush. *I no good at think talk.*

It's me, when I first came here. I feel like embracing them.

'I wasn't either.' I smile. 'It gets easier, with practice.'

'Are you one of the Settlers?' they ask nervously.

'No,' I say, 'I'm like you. Or I was, a suncycle ago. My name's Daghu-N.'

'Pith-Q,' they reply. 'What do you mean, you were like me a suncycle ago?'

'I lived in the Sanctuary.'

'But that's not possible!' Pith-Q says. 'The Guru's

only been here 30 senniths. You must be mistaken.'

I *could* point out the row of bulderbramble bushes, green flowers rippling gently in the breeze at the edge of the growth meadow but decide against it.

'I'm looking for Addh-C,' I say. 'Are they still here? They're half-Drahvvan, about so high, a couple of cycles older than me, they're… oh, look.'

I thoughtshare again, projecting an image of Addh-C directly into the Younger's mind. Their eyes widen.

'How did you do that?' they gasp.

'It'll come with practice.' I smile again. 'Do you know them?'

Pith-Q shakes their head.

'Oh. What about Ritch-U? Or Kayleb-J?'

Again, I thoughtshare faces. Again, they shake their head. I'm disappointed. Then something hits me: a sensation, or is it a memory? If it is, it doesn't belong to me. Or to Pith-Q apparently. It's a Byzhan in chains. Losing the strength in their limbs, numbness creeping through their body until it paralyses them completely. The walls of the room where they're being chained and drugged are filthy, blood-stained, mottled by the regular scrape of machinery. They're terrified. I see their face.

It's Addh-C. And I know where they are.

The Younger gasps as I hold my hand in front of the nutrition plant door and send blue energy fizzing into the locking mechanism.

'You can't go in there!' they exclaim.

'Who says so?' I sneer as the lock clicks, the door swings open. 'The Guru? They *lie*, Pith-Q!'

The room is cavernous, grimy, and definitely the one I saw in my vision. The smell hits us. It's not the one I expected—the sharp stink of rotting vegetable matter; this is far worse. It's the same stench I encountered when we found the decaying shortneck in the Broken Hemisphere, only more intense.

This place reeks of death.

It's where Addh-C died, I know it now. Ritch-U and the others all died here too. They were chained and drugged, like beasts in the slaughterhouses, then fed into the machines that line the walls, their bones crushed, their body fat melted into sludge that eventually left the building in pipes that fertilised the crops used to feed the next suncycle's worth of Not Like brought to the Sanctuary.

I turn to offer words of comfort to Pith-Q, but they've run away. It won't be long before Clahh-M is alerted to my presence, and I face the prospect of becoming fertiliser myself. I remember their cupboard full of trophies—Coell-J's medallion, my

Primary's gold pin—and realise the scale of their betrayal. If Coel-J was brought here back when I was a Younger, who's to say how long Clahh-M has been feeding Not Like into the soil?

I'm gripped with horror, rage, grief.

I raise my hand to send a wave of energy that will bring the tanks crashing to the ground, rip the pipes out of the walls, end this once and for all... but I can't. The energy will not come.

Byzhan Superiors are incapable of harming any living thing. That's what Addh-C told me. The sludge in those tanks was once living matter: Addh-C, my friends. Mine can't be the hand to destroy them, even in this state.

Addh-C is dead. They're dead.

I fall to my knees, weeping.

I want Mai-Mummh-E.

I don't know what the words mean yet, but I understand the feeling. *Your* feeling. And that's enough to take me where I need to go, see who I need to see.

48: Earth

Saturday 24th October, 2009

'You're telling me that dead thing under the playground is their *mother?*' Johnny asked incredulously. 'How the hell did you work that one out?'

Robert, who was clutching a large glass of juice (that, to his friends' astonishment, had appeared out of thin air on the circular table, apparently thanks to their friend on the PA) replied calmly:

'We were linked, telepathically. Only for a moment. Something to do with the fragment of time-space corridor.'

'Well of course it was,' said Johnny sarcastically. 'Sorry for asking, Mr Spock!'

He raised an eyebrow and sat next to Andy, who was staring at the creature, now safely imprisoned behind the forcefield again.

'What else did you sense,' Carol asked, 'if anything?'

'It was hungry,' Robert replied, 'very hungry indeed. I think that's why they've been draining people.'

'Why they've what?' Andy asked nervously.

'They haven't been eating people whole,' Carol explained. 'Just draining them of blood. There must be something in our blood that they need, something they get from their mother, perhaps?'

'Alien breast milk?' Johnny scoffed.

'Exactly!' said Robert. 'But there isn't enough of it in blood, that's why they've been eating other stuff—the warning signs and so on. They've been so desperate for food that they've created tunnels by… well, by eating the ground itself!'

'And the foundations!' Andy exclaimed, then, when prompted, explained what he'd observed about his improvised weapon. Gingerly, he handed it over to Carol, who placed it carefully on the circular table.

'Thank you, Andy,' the PA voice announced. 'That might be a vital key in handling the lassertilla.'

'Couldn't we just get a whole load of these guns and wipe the buggers out?!' Johnny suggested, toying with Carol's gun, 'Phasers set to kill, Captain?'

'Lassertilla?' Robert repeated, ignoring Johnny. 'You've identified them?'

'Yes, Robert, thanks to my recalibration. Unfortunately, this is a male of the species, so it lacks the ability to lactate. However, if I can isolate something missing from this stone that can also be found in human blood, we should be able to manufacture a compound that would satisfy the

177

lassertilla and stop them destroying Barcombe Hill and its inhabitants.'

'Like making baby formula?' asked Andy.

'Yes, Andy,' said the PA.

49: Barr-Byzhan

Dagre-Sunonh, Sennith 3/ 0, Suncycle Eftah

Their eyes are wide, bloodshot, terrified. At first, I barely recognise them; the Secondary I remember took care of their appearance, their clothes meticulously clean and uncreased. Their regulation face paint followed and emphasised their features to perfection. My fellow inculcatalists commented on it. But this Byzhan is wild, unkempt, their hair allowed to hang unnaturally from their scalp, their feet bare and grimy. They hammer their fists on the glass, mouth open in a soundless scream, tears, sweat and saliva mingling and splashing onto their already soaked, torn clothing.

I cross the corridor and touch the glass. For a moment they seem to recognise me, their mouth narrows, their head tips to the side. Their fists unfurl and fingers press the window as if they're trying to reach through it and touch mine. Fresh tears spring from their eyes. Are they mouthing my name?

Sec-sec, I thoughtshare, then think again, mouthing the word, my own eyes filling with tears. Then the fury returns, the tortuous silent scream begins again. They fling themself across the cell and into one of the walls.

My first sight of the Madness.

'But that's not possible, they're normal, we both are!'

I know the voice. I retreat into a recess further up the corridor.

'I've no doubt that you are a Creator-fearing Citizen, Daghu-T-Ollis,' another voice replies, getting closer. 'And, though your pairbonder appeared to show no signs of perversion when you pairbonded, I think you have to accept that you were deceived. The RAD447/Z disorder only infects the Not Like, we all know that.'

'But they're *normal!*' my Primary insists.

'The evidence says otherwise.'

They're standing outside the cell now. My Primary can't bring themself to look through the glass.

'I'm sure it must have occurred to you,' the second Byzhan continues, an Establishment official, judging by their uniform, 'when your pairbonder was unable to bear a Youngest... I assume they weren't, incidentally? The records for the allocated period seem to be corrupted.'

'Yes,' my Primary says quietly. 'I understand there was some sort of virus in the records system a little while ago?'

They're lying.

'These things happen.' The official sighs. 'Outer Island terrorists probably. Yours aren't the only records to have been corrupted.'

'We might have been unable to have Youngests,' my Primary lies, 'but that doesn't necessarily mean that my pairbonder was... *that way*.'

They can't even say it. It would seem that my Primary has become a terrorist, using their technical expertise to create an alternative reality where I wasn't born, rather than acknowledge that I'm Not Like. I feel sickened. Though I'm tempted to reveal myself and challenge the lie, I decide that rescuing my Secondary from this living hell is more important. Quite how I'm going to do it isn't immediately clear.

'Forget your pairbonder, Citizen Daghu,' the official advises. 'Go back to your life and make the most of it. We will take care of them. They will be transported to palliative facilities in the Broken Hemisphere that have been constructed specifically to treat those suffering from the RAD447/Z disorder. Establishmentor Hatch has, as you know, vowed to rid the world of both the disorder and the Not Like. You can be assured that your pairbonder will play their part.'

50: Earth

Saturday 24th October, 2009

It took barely an hour for TIM to isolate the nutrients needed to create the 'baby formula', and even less time to produce enough phials of it to place into hypodermic attachments to the stun guns for all four of them.

'I'm not sure about letting you come with us,' Carol said to Andy, as he clipped a gun onto his teleport belt.

'Are you kidding?!' Johnny shouted across from the jaunting pad. 'We've been stuck in this dump for *hours* now, I need to get out in the air!'

'Well, you're not going to get much of *that* in the tunnels,' Robert commented archly, stroking the surprisingly soft skin beneath the lassertillum's right ear. Perhaps because he'd been the one to inject the creature with the formula, it had immediately attached itself to him and was now purring contentedly, eyes half-closed, nuzzling its nose into his lap.

'You know what I mean,' Johnny replied softly, blushing faintly. Whilst TIM had been scanning and calculating, they'd all swapped life-stories. Since then, Johnny's anger at the world had apparently subsided. For the moment, at least.

'I think we'll manage okay,' Andy reassured Carol. 'We survived the killer pixies, then nearly two years of scavenging out there. Besides, if we can save lives doing this, I'm definitely up for it.'

'Yeah,' Johnny added, 'what he said.'

Carol nodded and stepped onto the jaunting pad. Robert prised the purring lassertillum off his leg and, picking up a modified stun gun, said, 'Look after Simon, will you, TIM?'

'Simon?!' Johnny repeated as Robert joined them on the pad.

'He looks like a Simon to me,' Robert replied as they vanished.

Three hours later they reappeared.

'We can get them back to Lassertil-6 just fine,' Carol was saying, 'if that's where they came from. The real question is, who brought them *here?* And why? TIM, have you been able to identify the logo on the signs around the village?'

'I have, Carol.'

The lassertillum squealed with pleasure as Robert approached it, picking up his half-drunk glass of nutrient juice on the way.

'The company it belongs to is…'

TIM's voice snapped off as a glass fell to the floor with a resounding smash. Once again Robert fell to his knees, the lights flickered out and the bluish energy enveloped him. He opened his mouth to scream.

51: Barr-Byzhan

Dagre-Sunonh, Sennith 3 / 0, Suncycle Eftah

If this place was built for palliative care, there's no sign of it. On the rare occasions that I've visited medical facilities in the past. I've been literally dazzled by their cleanliness: pristine white walls and floors that have been kept immaculately clean by buzzing anti-infection roboids. Equally spotless windows that let in the sunlight when it's needed but also provide soothing shade if the patient's temperature exceeds the acceptable limit for their recovery.

These walls are blackened with dirt, blood, Byzhan waste, The Creator knows what else. The 'patients' lie not in temperature-controlled sleeping pods but in roughly moulded caskets, crammed together, leaving no space for medics. Each patient is fastened into their casket by ugly black belts. My Secondary is straining against theirs, a guttural moan of despair muffled by a particularly tight belt around their mouth. Their groaning joins the terrible cacophony of terror that fills the room and makes me gag from the horror of it.

Though I'm three or four rows of caskets away from them, I manage to concentrate my energy on theirs and release their gag. I immediately regret it. My Secondary's scream, uninhibited now, chill me to the core.

And theirs is not the only scream I can hear.

52: The Corridor

Timeless

There was a corridor. A long corridor filled with dust and echoes of the dying. At its end, far, far away, the light was incandescent, so bright it blinded him. A shadow passed over the light, tiny at first. But then it slowly grew. The closer he got to the end of the corridor, the larger and more defined the shadow became.

It was a figure. A man saving him from the light. *James?*

Robert stopped screaming.

He stepped out of the light into the darkness and saw the face of the man who'd reached across time and space to find him, to rescue him. He reached out to touch it.

53: Barr-Byzhan

Dagre-Sunonh, Sennith 3 / 0, Suncycle Eftah

Robh-Erdmich-L.

I know your name now. I can see through your eyes; I can smell the salt of your tears and taste the residue of fruit on your lips. And more vivid than that is the memory of a scream—someone as close to you as my Secondary was to me—there's that name again: *Mai-Mumhh-E.* Are they your Secondary? Their name, like yours, is perverted, but maybe, like the Sups, you do things differently on your world.

Your world.

I try to reach further into your mind, see your world through your eyes, Robh-Erdmich-L, but all I get are flashes, images that are gone before I can fully grasp their meaning. A body—is it a body?—it's known to you, familiar from Younghood. Is it your Secondary? Your pairbonder? Are they screaming? Their skin is burning, a low throb of pain bursts from their belly and into the air. They shake, and the ground around them responds in kind. Connected. They must be Not Like. They have the Madness!

But this is the past. They're calm now, at peace. You've cured them. How did you do it, Robh-

Erdmich-L? Can we cure my Secondary in the same way? My skin tingles with hope.

You grasp my mind and lead me down the misty corridors of your memories and experiences to the cure.

And I see it. I understand it.

I know what I have to do now.

I can save Barr-Byzhan from the Madness.

54: Earth

Saturday 24th October, 2009

'It was James,' Robert sobbed. 'I saw James again! He's alive, Carol!'

'James?' Andy asked, his arm around his old school friend.

Johnny was standing on the other side of the Lab, watching silently.

'My boyfriend,' Robert replied, wiping his eyes. 'We thought he was dead. We thought he'd sacrificed himself to save… But that doesn't matter. We were wrong! He's alive, at the other end of that corridor, and he needs my help!'

The lassertillum, apparently oblivious to the emotional upheaval in the room, snorted and settled itself back into Robert's lap, its tail curling around Andy's ankles playfully.

'I'm coming back as one of those things!' Johnny joked halfheartedly, nodding towards it. 'All fur and purr when it's fed, then bites your head off as soon as it's hungry!'

Andy smiled weakly.

'I would advise against trying to enter the corridor fragment,' said TIM. 'Although it does seem to focus on you, my readings indicate that it's unstable. It moves. Even if you managed to travel along it, there's no guarantee that you could find your way back.'

'You remember what happened to Paul,' Carol added gently.

'I don't care!' Robert objected, 'I'm going!'

55: Barr-Byzhan

Dagre-Sunonh, Sennith 3/0, Suncycle Eftah

I know how placeroaming works now. I know where I must go, whom I have to see. I turn away from the caskets and focus on another face. It's one I know well from vidcasts but have seen only once in the flesh. Then it was impassive, disinterested, but

188

commanding, nonetheless. When they hear what I have to say, they will be far from disinterested. The information I have will save their world; I don't care if they take the credit for it (as they inevitably will)—all that matters is that we will rid Bar-Byzhan of the Madness.

Resisting the temptation to take one last glance back at my tortured Secondary, I hear the discordant music of the placeroaming growing to a crescendo…

…and I am standing in the cavernous boardroom of the Establishmentoral Palace. Directly in front of me is a familiar portrait—it can be found on the walls of every workplace in the Citadel and in the private living pods of those in strata high enough to merit an Artistic Representation Allowance. This is the original piece, though, its tones and colours more vivid than any reproduction, set off perfectly by the blackstone walls. It was either created a considerable number of suncycles ago, before the weight of Establishmentor Hatch's position began to take its toll on their face, or by artists given license to break the law and bend the truth.

I hear weapons powering up behind me and turn to see Establishmentor Hatch flanked by guards, all of whom have me in their sights. I raise my hands in surrender.

'Establishmentor…' I begin.

'Down on the floor, NOW!' one of the guards barks, but before I can oblige, Establishmentor Hatch, with a gentle flick of their right hand, commands that they lower their weapons.

'Placeroaming in the Establishmentoral Palace?' They sound bemused. 'Chancellor Ffilhips, have the dampeners developed a fault?'

One of the dignitaries sitting at the long table presses some buttons on the workplace in front of them, which bleeps in response.

'No, Establishmentor Hatch, they're working perfectly.'

'How interesting,' Establishmentor Hatch says, narrowing their eyes as they assess my clothing. 'A cleric, I take it? Are you here on official business from Their Holiness? I'd heard rumours that some of the monasteries were harbouring the Not Like but dismissed them as the wishful fantasies of non-believers. Perhaps we should mount an official investigation? It's about time we brought the Clericdom into line a little.'

'I'm not here on behalf of the Clericdom, Establishmentor Hatch,' I say. 'I've come here to give you some important information that could save Barr-Byzhan from the Madness!'

There is a heavy silence. A couple of the dignitaries swap glances.

'Oh really?' Establishmentor Hatch responds eventually. 'And would you care to explain exactly what this information might be, and how you came to find it?'

Their tone is slightly accusatory. It makes me nervous.

'My Secondary has the Madness,' I begin. 'I visited them in a medical centre in the Broken Hemisphere—and Establishmentor Hatch, if I were you, I'd have this one investigated; it was a dreadful place, filthy, inbyzhane...'

They're nodding. Is that a smile?

'You *visited* your Secondary, you say?'

'Yes. And I travelled inside them... I'm, uh, Not Like, you see...'

'We were aware of that. Do go on.'

'I was able to explore their organs, their blood, go deep inside their tissue, and what I saw there...'

'What you saw there were blood cells being consumed by gripp pollen,' a new voice pronounces from the doorway behind me. 'Very hungry gripp pollen, you might say, having been denied the enzymes they desired by the RAD447/Z virus. A virus that I helped create here in the Palace's

191

excellent laboratories. Hello, Daghu-N. I wondered what happened to you after you, uh, abandoned us.'

Clahh-M is dressed in an Establishment Official uniform, holding an infopad, which they hand to one of the dignitaries. Everything that happened on the Island makes sense to me now: the Establishment uses it to gather together the Not Like and destroy them. Or could it be only a radical section of the Establishment? Establishmentor Hatch seems as surprised as I am at Clahh-M's revelation.

'Establishmentor Hatch,' I say to them, 'this Byzhan is posing as a Not Like on one of the Outer Islands. Someone is trying to commit genocide—they want to wipe us out, I'm sure of it!'

'I think we've heard *quite* enough from you!' they snap. 'And as for you, Medic Clahh-M-Gogh, do I have to remind you that this is an Establishmentoral Chamber and therefore you are forbidden to speak?'

So the Establishmentor was not horrified by the true nature of the Madness but by one of their employees speaking out of turn!

'My apologies, Establishmentor Hatch,' Clahh-M-Gogh mutters, lowering their head and retreating from the chamber.

'Take this intruder to the nearest medical facility,' the Establishmentor orders one of the guards, 'and ensure that they are injected with the highest dose of dampening serum you can find. We can't have the perverteds placeroaming all over the place, can we? Not with another election coming up.'

56: Earth

Saturday 24th October, 2009

'Take care of yourself, mate,' Johnny smiled as Robert stepped onto the jaunting pad, stun gun in one hand and teleport belt in another.

'I hate it when people call me *mate*,' Robert replied.

'Sorry, Bobby,' Johnny said softly.

'Good luck,' Andy chimed in. 'Don't do anything we wouldn't do!'

'That doesn't leave much scope,' Robert quipped, then told TIM he was ready.

'Remember,' said Carol, 'there's a chance we might be able to communicate with you, even though TIM can't calculate where the fragment of corridor ends. Or when…'

'I know, Carol,' Robert reassured her, 'I'll try my best.'

'I know you will,' she said, then stepped up onto the pad to give him a hug, 'Good luck, Robert. Give my love to James.'

Robert grinned, took one final look at the Lab, and vanished.

57: Barr-Byzhan

Dagre-Lunh, Sennith 3/1, Suncycle Eftah

I'm dying, I know it. I can't move my limbs, open my eyes. I can barely breathe; my powers have gone. I have no way of knowing whether I'm in the same place as my Secondary or not. Have they put me in a casket to rot, like them?

It's so dark.

And silent.

And yet…

58: The Corridor

Timeless

This experience of the corridor was quite different to the one he'd had before. Though the walls, floor and ceiling had no substance as such—the corridor seemed to be formed entirely of buzzing, cobalt blue energy—it was somehow more tangible. More real. There was a forward motion, gradually gathering speed, propelling him towards its send, and James. The closer he got, the more certain Robert was that they were going to be reunited. A miracle, one might say.

James might say.

James. James Lanyon Kitto.

He projected his thoughts forward along the corridor, heart in his mouth, and found what he was looking for... James, lying naked and bruised in what looked like a coffin. Bound. Gagged. Eyes closed, hair longer than before, matted with blood. Sleeping? Or... No. He wouldn't lose him again. He wouldn't let him die again.

Robert reached out with his mind, reached out to the man he loved, the man who'd saved him from the darkness. He touched the bloody cheek, and James's eyes flickered open.

Alive!

He leant over, pulled the gag out of his lover's mouth, ready to lift him out of the coffin, and then, suddenly, he was actually standing in the room, or the cave, or whatever it was. He could smell the pungent odour of rotting manure, sweat dripped immediately from his forehead in the overwhelming heat.

And the cheek he was touching belonged to a lassertillum. A bruised and bleeding lassertillum, gazing helplessly up at him from one of at least a hundred caskets. Each with a dead or dying creature in them, all bound and gagged. The one he was touching, the one he'd mistaken for James, was looking at him now with a changed expression. One of recognition.

It opened its mouth to grunt a few indecipherable words—were they words? Its mouth and tongue moved as though they were. An alarm sounded somewhere: a harsh, pulsating, dangerous sound. Lifting the creature's emaciated body towards him, Robert gently encircled it with the teleport belt. Hoping for another miracle, he grabbed the lassertillum's arm with one hand and pressed his 'Safe Return' button with the other.

59: Barr-Byzhan

Dagre-Lunh, Sennith 3/ 1, Suncycle Eftah

You found me, Robh-Erdmich-L.

I don't understand, yet, what brought us together. Two different species—you've no tail, no jaw or neck to speak of—and yet you can thoughtshare and placeroam. What we can't share with language we can share with our minds. This idea you have about 'reincarnation'—is that the word?—sounds like Clericdom nonsense to me, but maybe the very fact that you're here points to the possibility of things beyond our comprehension.

We sit now in the place I have felt safest. The last time I was here, Addh-C was alive, their naked back facing away from me in the middle of the dark-cyc. You've seen the emblem, the same one that decorated the fertilisation plant on the Island. You recognised it, from your world.

But not of your world.

I feel at ease with you, Robh-Erdmich-L, and I believe you feel the same about me. But we both have questions that need answering, injustices that need addressing.

Do we solve them together?

It's a choice we have to make sooner or later. But maybe not quite yet.

You may also enjoy…

You may also enjoy…

ROGER PRICE'S
THE
TOMORROW
PEOPLE

IN
CHILDREN OF THE EVOLUTION
IAIN McLAUGHLIN